THE
EXTRAORDINARY
GARDEN

THE
EXTRAORDINARY
GARDEN

FRANÇOIS GRAVEL

A Novel

Translated by Sheila Fischman

Cormorant Books

The publisher gratefully acknowledges the support of the Canada Council for the Arts
and the Ontario Arts Council for its publishing program. We acknowledge
the financial support of the Government of Canada through the Book Publishing
Industry Development Program (BPIDP) for our publishing activities.

Printed and bound in Canada

NATIONAL LIBRARY OF CANADA CATALOGUING IN PUBLICATION

Gravel, François
[Je ne comprends pas tout. English]
The extraordinary garden: a novel /by François Gravel;
translated by Sheila Fischman.

Translation of: Je ne comprends pas tout.
ISBN 1-896951-53-8

1. Fischman, Sheilla II. Title. III. Title: Je ne comprends pas tout. English.

PS8563.R3888J4213 2004   C843'.54   C2004-904126-6

Editor: Marc Côté
Cover and text design: Tannice Goddard, Soul Oasis Networking
Cover image: Yellow Dog Production/Getty Images
Printer: AGMV Marquis

CORMORANT BOOKS INC.
215 SPADINA AVENUE, STUDIO 230, TORONTO, ONTARIO, CANADA M5T 2C7
www.cormorantbooks.com

THE
EXTRAORDINARY GARDEN

A LOVE STORY

I can sum up the whole story in two minutes, if you want: I desired her for seven years, I loved her for three days and three nights, and then I spent seven years trying to forget her. Don't worry, I'm not into numerology, and I have no plans to add a new chapter to the Bible. I'm simply taking advantage of this seventh anniversary to put an end to my silence; the reason I'm here is to tell you a love story that we swore we'd never disclose to anyone. Today, I've decided to speak: it's been seven years now, so who could be upset? The children have grown up, they're adults...

I think about her a lot, especially in the evening when I take my walk. I like to walk. For my health, to keep in shape, but also because I like the way my head operates when I walk for a long time: it's as if ideas are just waiting at the corner of a street or behind the trees, and if I want to meet them, I have to walk. Actually, most of the time when I think about her, I don't use ideas or even words, I use images. Now I suppose I'd have to add words to those images, wrap them up prettily, so I could store them tidily in a filing cabinet, and send them to the archives of the Ministry of Forgetting. I'd toss the key to the filing cabinet down a well and return home at last with a light heart. But the day after, full of regrets, I'd go down into the well to get the key back … Yes, that's what I'd do. I know myself.

In the filing cabinet there would be, for a start, certain smells. I just have to close my eyes and they come back, perfidious. Close my eyes, breathe deeply … The first time I kissed her, or rather the first time I touched her with my lips, was on the wharf in Baie-Comeau. I touched nothing but her clothes: I came up to her from behind, I put my hands on her arms to keep her prisoner, and I dropped a kiss onto her shoulder. It smelled of "delicate spring scent" or a "bouquet of freshly picked lavender," I can't say which — laundry soap and fabric softener smells — but then I moved closer to her neck and the smells became more liquid, more alive: toilet water and bath salts, face creams and shampoos, and finally her own perfume behind the others, beyond the others … And I could see her neck, the down on her neck, I could see it from so close that it was blurred, and it drove me crazy. I had waited seven years before I dared to touch her.

Seven years of secretly desiring her without ever being able to take that desire to its logical conclusion.

She, incidentally, is Josée. She lived on the other side of the nature park. If you're familiar with Longueuil, I'm sure you know what I'm talking about: from my house, on cross-country skis, it just takes two or three strides to gain access to the local park; her backyard opened onto it too, but at the other end. We lived in the city but we just had to walk through a forest in order to pay one another a visit. A magical forest. An "extraordinary garden," in the words of Trenet's song. Our secret garden smelled of snow and dead leaves, of earth and spruce trees. And because of the children, there were also the smells of licorice, of vinegar chips, of wet mittens …

There are children in this story. Four children. Josée is married. So am I, for that matter. We live in the same neighbourhood, our children are the same age, we run into each other on the playground, at the rink or the mall, but it will take a good while before we realize that ours is a love story, and even longer — an eternity — before we finally decide to let that story come true, before I drop a kiss on her shoulder and dare to move closer to her neck …

Separate marriages, separate houses, but a big backyard in common, an extraordinary garden where I see Josée appear along a path. It's her face that I see first, in close-up, like on a movie screen. I see her in IMAX, but as time passes, the image gets more and more hazy. Or increasingly simple, rather, like the doctored or air-brushed photos used in ads: you see her hair and her eyes, and that's all. Her hair is very fine, very straight. She tried all sorts of ways to make it curl, but nothing worked. She must have tried a dozen different cuts and thirty-six different products to give it body, but to no avail. Finally, she had it cut very short. In the winter, when she took off her headband, it was all tousled, and that made her resemble a pixieish teenager, the farthest thing from a mother. I felt as if that look was just for me, I felt as if I was stealing it from her life.

It would be hard for me to describe her eyes. If I said that they were brown with hints of green, you wouldn't be much further ahead. A person has to try to describe someone's eyes — or anything else — to realize how much vocabulary we lack, but never mind: while I can't describe their exact colour, at least I can tell you that you need only look at those eyes to feel that life could be something very wonderful. If I let myself go, I'd talk about gentleness, about benevolence. I would look at those eyes and tell myself it's true, there really are women who look at their children that way, women who see life through eyes like that. And I wanted those eyes to look at me closely, to watch over me.

I've never seen her again. Except in a dream, a dream I've had so many times that I can no longer distinguish between it and reality.

Seven years later, all I have left is a face that I call up from my memories. It rises in my memory as in a glass elevator

—
4

and I see again, first of all, her hair, like a halo, and then her eyes ... The rest disappears and every piece that disappears hurts me a little more, leaves me a little more alone, a little chillier.

But why don't I tell you a little about myself before I get my story underway? That's where I should have started, I think: I arrive at your house, I settle in, and I start to tell you my love story ... My name is Marc-André Fillion and I'm forty-seven years old. No handicaps, no chronic illness, no distinguishing characteristics, as the cops would say. I walk a lot, I keep in shape. Cross-country skiing, cycling, swimming, hiking; I burn calories conscientiously, but I still consume a few more, and the laws of physics being what they are ... You know how it is after a certain age ... I eat a little too much, I enjoy fine wine, but not to excess.

There's a risk that I'll be seriously boring if I tell you about my work, but so it goes: I'm the head of purchasing and real estate with Human Resources. Just imagine the forms, the furniture, the computers and telephone systems needed to keep six thousand employees busy, not to mention the buildings that have to be rented or bought: all that passes through my hands. I'm talking about budgets, obviously. I've been working here for twelve years. Before that, I was with Revenue.

Six thousand individuals, that's right. It takes six thousand individuals to find jobs for the rest. That makes at least six thousand who don't need to hunt for jobs ... And by the way, would you believe me if I told you that in twelve years I haven't seen a single trace of a jobless person? I work in a closed office downtown, with my computer and my administrative assistant. I sign papers, I authorize purchasing budgets, I reshuffle flow charts ... The real beneficiaries, I don't know. To me, they're pure abstractions. At the office when people talk about those who are in direct contact with the jobless, they say that they're on the front lines. That expression always makes me flinch. It sounds military, don't you think? The front line, the line of fire ... As if our civil servants were lying in the mud of the trenches under enemy mortar fire, when they actually work in offices, cozy and warm ... But to come back to my own job: if the public service were an army, I wouldn't even be a general. Generals still have to fight now and then; they go to the front, some of them even die. Picture instead a large office, very far from the battlefield. In that office, an army of accountants is calculating the cost of the machine guns, ammunition, gas masks. My job is to manage those accountants. As you can see, we're a long way from the line of fire.

So I work in a big office, downtown. Bureaucracy, heaviness, frustration, politics — all the horrors you can imagine in a place like this, but I still feel that I'm doing important work, that I'm a competent employee. I get paid to make decisions, so I make them. I like to think that I'm a responsible manager, who has the taxpayers' interests at heart ...

I'm straining the elastic of your patience, right? Don't protest, I'm used to it: if I were a Formula 1 driver or an explorer, I could talk shop for hours. But a manager, especially one who works for the government…

It's what I always wanted to do. In high school I was the kind of pupil who got good grades in every subject but was never a champion, never did anything remarkable, you know what I mean? *Rule-oriented*, as they say in English. Ask me to solve an equation with two unknowns and I'm your man. Give me ten pages worth and I'll deliver the goods the next morning, without fail. But don't ask me what it's good for, and in particular, don't ask me to take it a little farther. Whether it's French or physics, history or chemistry, it's the same difference. Show me procedures and I proceed. And I get good grades: 75, 80 … In high school, I had no idea about a vocation, even less about a career plan. I just had to come across a good chemistry teacher and I wanted to be a chemist, a French teacher who was the slightest bit interesting and I wanted to become a French teacher.

In college I was still "rule-oriented," so much so that I studied pure science because the guidance counsellors had urged me to. I still racked up 75s and 80s but I didn't really like it. Which was too bad for the guidance counsellors, but I didn't enjoy balancing equations. I went on to the end anyway because people expected me to, and I finally discovered that there's one field especially designed for those with marks around 75 or 80 who don't want to specialize and confine themselves to the same problems forever: management. The chemist is a chemist for life; the French teacher too; but the administrator can work just as well in the private sector as in the public, in a multinational or a small business, in a petrochemical complex or an avant-garde theatre. He has to learn a bit of psychology, show some diplomatic skill, acquire a smattering of culture — which has never hurt anyone; he has to know his way around numbers without being a math genius, know something about books without trying to outdo Victor Hugo: in other words, become a well-rounded man, as they used to say ... And so I chose management and I've never regretted it.

Actually, I followed the road laid out by my older brother. Benoît studied management and now he's a university professor, in the department of Industrial Relations. My brother's marks were always around 90 or 95. When he got to university, he collected A's and A-pluses. He enjoys knowledge for its own sake. He's a seeker. Never satisfied. Whereas I specialized in the B's: B-plus, B-minus, B period. Accounting, finance, marketing — it was all the same. I enjoyed what I was learning, it all struck me as clear, neat and tidy, reasonable, practical, useful; but I had no desire to go further in the subject, go beyond its limits, explore. What I wanted to do was apply it, here and now and right away. To tell you the truth, what I most wanted was to finish school. To start working. And so I chose the civil service. For the security, I suppose, because it was the easiest path, but also as a reaction: my father had a furniture store on St. Hubert Street. Business was good in the 1950s and 1960s, but after that came a long slump, a slow bankruptcy that stretched over two decades ... Most likely that's why I wasn't drawn to a small private firm. To spend my whole life working and find myself at fifty with no future didn't appeal to me. So I finished my B.A. in management in 1975, and got a job right away in Revenue. I spent thirteen years there, first as auditor, then as supervisor; after that came a relocation as we say — "move" would be too simple — and as I had no desire to live in Shawinigan, I applied for a job in Manpower. First taxes, then unemployment. As you can see, I like guaranteed winners.

I seem to be straying from my subject, I know, but not that much, as you'll see.

So, I was saying that I liked guaranteed winners. Whatever I wanted, I got. A good salary, absolute job security, and just enough challenges to keep from being bored to death. As soon as I'd familiarized myself with all my cases I asked for a promotion and got it. When I wanted to take advanced classes, my tuition was paid. And meanwhile, I rose through the ranks quite serenely, without taking shortcuts. A good job that allowed me to concentrate on the essential things. And for me that meant the wife I had and the children I would have. If I was in such a hurry to leave university, it was so I could live my family life to the full.

I think I can truly say that I'm a family man; yes, fiercely, absolutely a family man. If I hadn't been so fiercely a family man I probably wouldn't be here now, telling you about Josée. I would have gone away with her and that would have been that ... But we can't always choose the endings we want, can we?

AND HOW'S THE FAMILY?

*E*veryone has three families: the one we're subjected to, the one we choose — or think we choose — and the one we dream about while we're strolling the paths of the extraordinary garden.

In the family I come from, there's a silent father who works six days a week, ten or twelve hours a day. A father who works very hard, all his life, so he can afford a house for his family. A suburban house with trees and clean air, a house he paid for with thousands of hours of work, that he gives to his wife and children because he can't imagine a finer gift. Since nobody wants that house, he makes do with a chalet. Which is no more successful …

In the house of my childhood, there is also a mother. A mother cooped up in a house that to her is a prison.

A disgruntled mother who expresses herself more eloquently with sighs than with words. A mother who can't make her children feel welcome in a house that she doesn't like, in a life that she hasn't chosen. A frustrated mother, but who eventually transforms herself late in life: when she goes back to the job market in her forties, it's as if she's had a blood transfusion. Before, she was in black and white. After, she's in colour. And my father is the one who turns pale, who fades…

Disgruntled as a mother, happy when she no longer is: makes for a wonderful childhood.

As for my chosen family, Marie-France and I often compare it to a business. I know, that's not very romantic, but let me explain. For those who've studied management, there's nothing pejorative about the word — on the contrary: a business is first of all a dream, a crazy dream that you keep alive through sheer willpower, through patience, through work. While there's nothing easier than setting up a business, starting one that lasts is another matter. And a family has to last, otherwise what good is it? So, Marie-France and I had set up a family. It was our dream, our project. It became our business. A business that's still running, come hell or high water.

Finally, there is the third family. The family *that might have been* …

I'll tell you about the first time, okay? The very first time I saw Josée, on July 2, 1986. I remember the date because Marie-France and I had just bought the house on Lacombe

Street. We've just arrived in the area and we're exploring the neighbourhood with the children: little Marie, whom we often call "Just Plain Marie," is five years old, and Mathieu is three. It's hot that day, very hot. We go for a walk in the nature park, and as soon as Marie spots the ponds, she wants to swim. That child is a fish, she really is. It's inborn, I think: she sees water and her eyes dilate, her skin tingles; if we don't watch out — splash! — she's in the water ... Marie is five and she wants to swim in the ponds in the park. I try to stop her by explaining that these ponds are strictly ornamental, but she insists. When she gets something in her head ... Her sign may be Pisces the Fish, but with Pig Head ascendant. She wants to go in swimming and that's that; she can't imagine that ponds have been put in a park *just to look at*.

What can I tell her? That the police will arrest her? That the ponds are infested with radioactive leeches? I can't promise her that we'll go back to the house and buy a new swimming pool: we've just moved in, we've already spent a lot of money, and besides, you shouldn't make promises like that to children ... While I'm trying to be a proper parent — in other words, when I can't come up with an answer for her — she stamps her feet: I want to go in, I want to go in ... And then, all at once, a miracle. An apparition. Amélie.

Imagine a bundle of blonde curls and ribbons with two big blue eyes in the middle: that's Amélie. Between her and Marie, a lightning flash. And they're off: chattering, trading ponies, trading tricks for braiding their ponies' manes ...

In case you aren't familiar with them, these ponies are rubber horses. Pink and blue horses, with big Walt Disney eyes and fluorescent manes you have to brush. The big deal for little girls their age was brushing their ponies.

So we have Marie and Amélie trading pony brushes, while two little boys size each other up out of the corners of their eyes. These two are younger and a little warier. A question of temperament. Their connection isn't so quick: it takes two minutes, maybe three, before they're old friends. By their measure, three minutes is forever … But they'll soon be inseparable: remote-controlled cars, hockey cards, the neighbourhood school … Another few years and Alex will be goalie of the hockey team and Mathieu his most reliable defenceman. The girls and their ponies, the boys and hockey: I know, it reeks of cliché, but offer Alex or Mathieu a pony and he'll use it as a ball, give Marie or Amélie a fire-engine and she'll try to comb the ladder. It's not my fault, you see, if boys are boys and girls are girls.

Before we move on, here's a trick in case you have trouble remembering names: Marc-André marries Marie-France, and they have two children, Just Plain Marie and Mathieu. It was the priest at Mathieu's christening who observed that we're partial to the letter M. We hadn't even noticed. The M's, then, are mine. And the A's are Josée's. Two girls and two boys the same age, only weeks apart; two boys and two girls who have just moved into the neighbourhood and who decide, all four at once, to turn our lives upside down.

When you have children, you can forget about choosing your own friends. You may have perfectly delightful and charming neighbours whom you'll never get together with, you won't even know they exist; but if there are children twelve blocks away the same age as yours, you'll soon be sitting around their parents' table over coffee, discussing the relative importance of nature versus nurture while you wait for the lords and masters to finish their game of Monopoly. It's the children who choose their parents' friends. Real tyrants. Whom we obey. And we're perfectly happy to do so.

The children, then, are in their world and two adult couples are face to face, a little uncomfortable ... He is Robert. He's a policeman. But forget the clichés — the Dunkin' Donuts, the pot belly, the nightstick — that's not him at all. Robert is tall and slim, without an ounce of fat. Calm, with a deadpan, slightly British sense of humour ... What we like to imagine as British, that is: the stiff-upper-lip kind, not the hooligans ... In fact, Josée nicknames him Bobby, because of Robert of course, but also because of that English side to him. I'd like to tell you that he's dull and stupid, totally insensitive, and that he inhibits Josée from realizing her potential, but Robert is a really nice guy, I can't do anything about it. An exemplary father. The father you'd wish for any child on earth. His own kids adore him. So do mine. And Josée loves her Bobby, you can see it, feel it. He's impossible to hate, which is too bad.

Now let me introduce myself: I'm Marc-André Fillion, I've just moved into the neighbourhood, I work for Revenue Canada ... Coincidence: Robert works for the Sûreté du Québec, in the economic crimes division. He studied management and knows some of my colleagues well: what's become of So-and-so? In other words, we're off. Combing our ponies.

I've kept Josée for dessert, obviously. Narrator's privilege. Josée is a high-school librarian. For two high schools, in fact: it's rare that a school can afford one full time. She and Marie-France, who works in insurance, have nothing in common. They aren't on the same wavelength, but there's no animosity either ... I'll come back to that later, if you don't mind. For now, Josée turns to me, we shake hands ... I still remember the touch of her hand, which I thought was strangely cool, given the scorching heat. Later on, I found out that she had circulatory problems: her hands were always cold, her feet, too, for that matter, which could be ... startling. So I remember the touch of her hand, and I also remember that I hadn't looked at her the way a man would.

You know, the kind of look that checks out the goods, that thousandth of a second when you look at a woman for the first time and you wonder if the door will be open or shut. With Josée the question didn't even arise: she had young children, so did I. And to be honest, she wasn't particularly pretty. Not ugly either — no, far from it — but, let's say, acceptable. Rather short and a little hefty, actually. Not fat, no, but a heavy frame … None of which really mattered: what was most important was her open, luminous smile, and her cascading laughter … Josée was the kind of woman whose company you seek out, with whom you enjoy laughing and talking, but who doesn't have an ounce of sex appeal, you see what I mean? Certain women have a gift for emphasizing assets they don't even possess, of catching your eye, of exciting … Josée was very attractive, but in a different way. The kind of woman whose company you seek out without even being aware of it. My children went to her spontaneously, as if she were a big sister, a big sister who knew how to play, to listen, to console, without ever passing judgement. It was a good while before I found myself alone with her — there were always children around us, not to mention our legitimate spouses — but still, from the very beginning, I felt a strange intimacy. As if we were alone in the midst of all these people.

With her I had the impression I was going from one surprise to another. There are people who think things over like ruminants, others who are like moles; she was more like a mountain goat leaping from one summit to the next, elusive. Each of her replies, her retorts or her reflections, left me off balance, and I was never in a hurry to get back on my feet. With her, I didn't notice the time pass; she had the knack of making me laugh often, smile nearly all the time, surprise me always. And she was just as able to move me through small gestures, little things: the way she ran her hand through her children's hair, the words she found to console them, simple words that were just short of hokey, but that always rang true...

You must be familiar with that strange sensation you experience sometimes when you hear a brand new pop song on the radio, but you feel as if you've known it forever. Five or six notes, three chords on a guitar: you wonder through what miracle that song — which is so simple, so obvious — has never been composed before. You just hear it once and it stays in your head for the rest of your days. Josée was a song: I'd never seen her before but I knew her, recognized her. And as for staying in my head, well ... But I'm going too quickly, much too quickly. For the time being there's none of that: each of us had our family and we exchanged handshakes in the middle of the extraordinary garden.

It's a funny thing though, memory: nothing happened that day, absolutely nothing. I don't know if she and I exchanged two words. I talked mostly with Robert, actually. Nothing happened, yet when I run the scene again I can feel it down to the smallest detail: the humid summer air, the coolness of her hand, even the rustling of the leaves ... Nothing happened, practically nothing. Just two hands that touch. And Marie-France who's watching...

I could always try to rewrite the story, ask myself what would have happened if Josée and I had been alone that day, and if we'd been a few years younger, and if we hadn't had children, and if there hadn't been those ponds where Marie wanted to swim, and if the pony craze hadn't existed … And the truth is, we'd probably never have met. The children were part of it, from the word go. And Robert, and Marie-France. It's a complicated story, a story with four children and four grown-ups trying to be adults … That reminded you of the Jacques Brel song, didn't it? *To grow old without being an adult?* What we wanted was to be adults without growing old. Makes sense, doesn't it? Look around you and tell me if it was wrong for me to want to make a success of a family, to want to be an adult.

So, back to my story. As the children are still playing, we go on chatting, and soon we're in their backyard, drinking our beer or white wine or apple juice, and talking about the advantages of heat pumps and the best way to clean synthetic resin garden furniture. Suburban small talk. Respectful of the elementary rules of courtesy, we don't hang around for too long. But how can you separate children from their new friends, how can you tear them away from their new toys — which are the same ones they have at home? Though we swear that they'll see one another again, we are treated to cries, tears, heartbreak. To calm them down, we have to promise that maybe they'll get together again the next day, which doesn't seem to reassure them all that much: how can we convince them that *tomorrow* really exists, that it's not another of those boring lengths of time that adults specialize in? Tomorrow, later, when you're a grown-up …

Finally, they accept our arguments. Promises and hand-shakes, and Josée's cool hand in mine, once again, and Marie-France, watching...

ELLIPSIS

*Y*ou know what couples are like: always talking about other couples. It's their drug, their nourishment. That first evening, once the kids are in bed, Marie-France and I talk about Robert and Josée. Marie-France says that she likes Robert and that she's delighted the children have made some new friends so quickly, but she doesn't want us to get too close to them, or feel that we have to spend all our Saturday evenings together, either at their place or at ours. I think she's a little too anxious to set limits: there are no obligations, let's give them a chance, we got along well with them, and the risk that they'll turn into leeches strikes me as minimal ...

A moment later, the cat has left the bag: Marie-France says that of course Josée is very likeable, cheerful, amusing and all that, *but* …You know, the kind of *but* that you stretch out a little at the end of a sentence, and follow with an ellipsis. When I try to get her to clarify what she means by that *but*, she changes the subject, and not very subtly either. Usually, Marie-France has a knack for changing direction subtly, just like that, so that you don't realize it till the next day — if you do realize it. I try to pick up the thread, but she's doubly uncomfortable at being caught red-handed changing the subject, and she gets lost again in her ellipsis.

Needless to say we've had this kind of minor misunderstanding before — after all, we've been married for over ten years — but it is the first time the issue has something to do with mutual acquaintances. Usually we have the same affinities, the same hesitations, and for a long time now we've made no distinction between her friends and mine, or even between our two families. We often have dinners to which everyone's invited, friends as well as brothers-in-law and sisters-in-law, and a good time is had by all. Instead of falling silent, I keep at it — and I'm sure it's significant that I don't let go: no one's forcing us to eat at their place every week, but it could be nice now and then, and Josée strikes me as vivacious, engaging, amazing …

Sure, replies Marie-France, more and more prickly, sure she's very nice, *but* …

The thought seems very odd, but I ask her anyway: are you by any chance a little jealous?

"Maybe, yes," she replies without looking me in the eyes, which is not like her.

"You, jealous?"

For a minute, I must have looked like a fish in an aquarium. Mouth open, unable to talk, I listen to her tell me that it's a hunch, just a hunch, but she has a feeling that there's something going on between Josée and me, some kind of natural complicity that makes everyone else feel as if they're in the way, and that this is the first time she's felt anything like it ...

I knew that Marie-France was more fragile than she seemed — Marie-France is very beautiful, and we often think that beautiful women can't possibly have any problems, as if their psychological makeup is as harmonious as their features — but I thought she was strong where that's concerned. Never had I detected an ounce of jealousy in her, never.

We talk about it for a while before agreeing that her fears are ridiculous and then we go to sleep on it.

༈

Marie-France had always been suspicious of Josée, from the first day, and that suspicion would have some perverse effects: since it was always somewhat awkward when I talked about Josée at home, I avoided the subject. Nothing had happened between us, absolutely nothing, and already I felt illicit. Watch out now, I didn't say guilty: let me remind you that seven years would pass before I dared to touch her hair, before I dared to brush her shoulder with my lips. I don't feel guilty, no, but clandestine. I am a clandestine passenger on a ship that has just left the harbour, but I'm not aware of that yet. I head out to sea without knowing the destination of the ship. Towards ellipsis. Towards the extraordinary garden.

INTRODUCTION TO THE BUSINESS

T met Marie-France in 1972, at university. Picture two hundred and fifty students sitting in an auditorium for their very first management class, and a hundred and twenty-five of them — the guys — stop breathing when Marie-France makes her entrance and takes a seat in the front row. The others — the girls — go on chattering, chattering a little louder even, to mask their jealousy.

That's hardly an exaggeration: Marie-France is extremely beautiful. A long fluid body, with curves in the right places, and a natural elegance, a smoothness to her movements that make everything she wears look wonderful on her, even jeans — *especially* jeans. She comes from a well-to-do family and it shows: the sun always shines on her, everything seems to come easily. I look at her and already I'm congratulating myself on deciding to study management: let's hope for the most boring classes possible so I can spend all my time looking at her. That girl is a feast for the eyes, thank you God. So beautiful that I can sense a door closing from the first milli-second: that girl is not for you. You can look but you can't touch. So I look and I don't touch. Forget it, man: you don't live in the same world, you don't speak the same language, you don't breathe the same air. You could never take her skiing at Whistler or diving in the Caribbean or even invite her to play tennis. Marie-France seems to be the type who'd show up on the court in her little white skirt, you see, and her designer polo shirt. I'd be in jeans and holding my racquet like an axe. And she'd beat me effortlessly. She is the girl who's reserved for the quarterback, in a game where I can't even aspire to play defensive wing. I'd rather be a simple spectator: I look at her, I want her, like any normal male, but I never would have dared …

The truth is that I didn't have to make a move: she's the one who came looking for me.

We're at the end of our first year of university. Because we go to the same classes and the same cafeterias, inevitably we end up talking, even working on the same team. Nothing simpler than being her teammate, in spite of what you may think: far from throwing themselves at her, most of the guys avoid her. Beauty like hers is intimidating. So I get to know her, and I discover a girl a lot more amiable than I'd have thought at first. Less complicated, more accessible. Less and less a Barbie, to be honest. But as for imagining I could walk in Ken's shoes…

She has an apartment near the university, and one evening in April five or six of us are there, ostensibly to finish an assignment, but mainly for the pleasure of being together, of letting the time go by — university's useful for that too. There's pizza, a few beers, maybe a joint gets passed around (don't think that management students are any different from others; the jeans may be a little cleaner, that's all); we're five or six students, all in our early twenties, talking about this and that … The conversation soon turns to relationships — to marriage, more specifically. Marriage as an institution, more precisely as a bourgeois institution. Remember, this is the early 70s, a time when, unless you're totally out of it, no one would dare admit they were dreaming of marriage and bungalows, suburbs and fidelity. That's what I am doing, though, on the night in question, I'm even laying it on a bit thick: I'm dreaming not only of a family and a bungalow in the suburbs, but also of a little guy I'll drive to hockey on Saturday morning, and a little girl who'll take piano lessons, and a red, white and blue beach ball on a green lawn, and even a station wagon in the driveway — this is before the cult of the minivan.

This leads of course to a tremendous discussion. Voices are raised, arguments burst out, but the debate stays civilized, it always is with us: though we're only aspiring managers, we already have the polish of pros. Managers, like psychologists, abhor conflicts. They're taught to negotiate, always negotiate, and never turn anyone against you. Any contact may prove useful, any individual may one day be transformed into a client or supplier. And, who knows, maybe even a friend. *Human Being, Handle with Care*, as my Human Resources prof always used to say. So we have a little bit of a row, but courteously. We call each other diehard reactionary or revolutionary vermin, but deferentially.

While the girls say nothing.

When the group breaks up, around midnight, I'm there alone with Marie-France. No calculation on my part, I swear. Instead it was she who manoeuvred, as she'll confess to me later. No sooner has the door shut on the final guest than I'm trying to find a pretext for sneaking out. But she sits beside me, tells me she thought I was brave, that she likes my opinions and the way I stand up for them, and here she is tossing compliments at me. It's flattering, it makes me weak and sweet and warm. It goes to my head, and I'm not quite so anxious to leave, especially because she comes even closer, speaks to me more and more softly, until I finally understand that I just have to make a move, one little move … But I'm paralyzed. I didn't see it coming and I still can't believe it … Marie-France moves even closer, her lips are on mine … She thought I was quite awkward that night. And that my performance wasn't up to expectations, to tell the truth. But you have to understand me: Marie-France! Marie-France and me! As if such a thing could be possible!

I slept at her place that night. Didn't sleep, actually: I watched her sleep while I asked myself what had happened for me to end up there, in her bed, in her life, how could I have been teleported to another galaxy without my realizing … After that, I studied the ceiling, then I turned back to her: she was still there, I hadn't been dreaming, and I looked at her, stunned.

Days and weeks go by and she's still there, and I'm still just as incredulous, as if I'd hit the jackpot without even buying a lottery ticket.

Do I love her? I don't even ask myself: when heaven sends you such a gift you don't haggle over details. You accept it and that's that. And tell yourself that in any event, it won't last, it can't last.

I'm so proud to walk beside her along the university corridors and down the aisle at the movies, proud to introduce her to my parents, proud to detect a hint of envy in the eyes of my brother and my friends, proud to see people stare when we walk by … Proud that a girl like her has chosen me, me, proud that a girl has chosen me period. The best thing about it is that I'm not even jealous. Maybe because deep down I don't believe it: I keep expecting Ken to bounce back and take off with her in his white Corvette to go skiing at Whistler. But when Ken does bounce back, I'm the one she chooses, the one she chooses once again.

EXCHANGE OF SERVICES

*K*en's name is Normand — a fairly tacky name, I have to say, but you aren't obliged to share my taste in names. A past love, an affair that was never really ended, was dealt with badly, that I'd heard about a few times. I wasn't really surprised to see him bounce back right in the middle of our first summer.

Normand has a fabulous tennis racquet, elegant white shorts that are always impeccably pressed, and gorgeous biceps that are always impeccably bulging. He wants to play a few sets with Marie-France. Marie-France resists a little, but not for long. She tells me, Give me a little time, I know it's hard on you, but it's the only way I can ...

I knew it would happen sooner or later, I also knew that she was too beautiful for me, but at the same time I couldn't just give up: it had lasted three months, which proves that it's possible, right? Why should I give up without a fight, for what reason would I throw in the towel? But what can I do to hold on to her? Love can't be commanded, and it's no use threatening, clinging, or trying to convince her ... Since she's asking for time, I give her time: do what you have to, work for the best, you know what's at stake ...

I live through two months of scorpions devouring my belly, two sleepless months of waiting, two months of heavy drinking to knock myself out.

Every time I think she's gone for good, she comes back; every time, she shows that she cares about me; every time, she cries; every time, we talk for hours; and what can you do when a girl cries and asks you to wait, especially if that girl is Marie-France and her beauty brings tears to your eyes? You wait. You don't sleep, you drink too much and you wait. And it goes on like that for two months, then one night, a night when she's supposed to be with him, she comes back for good, she tells me it's over, she tells me I'm the one she's chosen. I never tried to find out if she was the one who'd called it off or he was, or what the reasons were. She had come back, she'd come back for good, that was all that mattered.

That was the night we decided to stay together, to marry, have children, set up a partnership whose name would be family.

In October we found an apartment near the university; the following May we got married. A real wedding, in a church. A real wedding with bouquets and corsages, wedding cake and marriage vows. Even the priest couldn't get over it.

Maybe it took the episode with Normand to make me realize that I loved Marie-France, and how much. For the first time in my life I could tell a girl, I love you, as often as she wanted to hear it, and know I was telling the truth. Before Marie-France, I never knew. If I said it anyway, I never knew if it was true until long after the breakup. Before Marie-France, I was always a man in love after the fact. With her, I loved the future and I couldn't imagine my future any way but with her.

I had time to discover that Marie-France was not only beautiful, she was also funny, generous, easy to get along with, uncomplicated … No latent defects, no artifice. Her nature was as harmonious as her features, if that's possible, but she was far more sensitive than I'd have thought, far more fragile. She needed me to be strong and I didn't mind that at all. Never would I have thought that it was possible to have so many complementary interests.

Like the children of actors, who so often become actors too, she was heading quite naturally for insurance: her father was a broker. While still at university she already had summer jobs with insurance companies. When she finished her degree she continued along that road. She quietly rose in the ranks, without cutting corners, then she stopped at the place she wanted to be, exactly the place she wanted to be. She had set herself as an objective a certain level of salary and responsibilities, which she quickly attained. For her, that wasn't the main thing. The main thing was the family. Hockey, piano, beach ball on the lawn, station wagon in the driveway ... If love means two people looking in the same direction as the saying goes, well, that certainly applied to us. Our eyes were fixed on the same horizon.

Oh yes, I loved Marie-France. I loved her as much as I thought it was possible to love until I met Josée.

PHOTOCOPIES

*T*here's one point I'd like to make right away. I want to tell you a story, in fact. A very ordinary story, slightly cheap and pathetic, something that happened during an office party back when I was working in the Revenue department. There was this girl, Jocelyne, who'd most likely been drinking a little that night — you know what office parties are like — and who was sending me signals so lacking in subtlety that I picked up on them. And there we were in the photocopy room … No need for details, I don't think, or for learned semantic distinctions between what is and isn't sexual.

What I want you to know is that I had a fleeting thought for Normand that night.

Revenge? That's a little strong. I'm sure it's true that revenge is a dish best served cold, but it shouldn't be kept around until it rots: this happened five years later, at least.

I told Marie-France. Without going into detail, obviously, and without drawing a connection with Normand. I told her about it because I owed her the truth, because I always told her everything. For those matters, we quickly establish a solid jurisprudence: we tell each other everything, absolutely everything.

There was a chill, certainly, but things were soon back to normal. We were married, we'd wanted children for a long time, we certainly weren't going to throw all that away because of a ... Because of a question of circumstances.

It was the only time, the one and only time.

It's a sad story, a bit pathetic, but I wanted to tell it because it's the truth. I'm no angel, I'm not trying to show myself in the best light, and I really don't like to play the victim. And I also want you to know that if I was so attracted to Josée, vengeance had nothing to do with it.

A LITTLE MORE BLUE,
FOR THE SKY

I know aggressive cyclists who eat up the pavement, fill their lungs with carbon dioxide, and draw a fine line of mud on their backs. A person might think these guys pedal just to lay on the stress. And don't even mention joggers: if they smile, it's for the gallery, to show that it doesn't really hurt, or rather, that they are courageously overcoming their pain. I suffer, therefore I exist ... But have you ever met up with an aggressive walker?

In the extraordinary garden there are kilometres of cross-country ski trails, and the people who walk there may not be totally happy — that would *really* be an extraordinary garden — but they're quietly contented, which is already a good reason to go there. You meet people who are walking, taking it easy, doing something that's good for them. They're relaxed, they're smiling, and it makes you want to smile back. Walking lets you clear your ledgers, lets you remove your inner accountant. The term doesn't exist, but it ought to. The opposite too, for that matter: when I see certain performers on television, I tell myself they ought to update their ledgers now and then. Oh, being creative is all well and good, but having both feet on the ground can come in handy too. Even if it's just for walking.

Imagine the look on a Japanese, a Chinese or even a French person if I told him that I live ten minutes from downtown, but if I get up early enough in the morning I may surprise deer having breakfast in my vegetable garden and raccoons raiding my garbage cans. In the yard just behind my house, I have access to a forest that's crisscrossed with paths. And at the end of those paths is Josée ...

But let's not cut corners: at the end of the path there are Josée *and* Robert *and* the children. And anyway, it's not me who wants to see Josée the next day, it's Just Plain Marie, who absolutely insists on going back to the ponds, *where we aren't allowed to go in swimming but it's where Amélie is*. My daughter imagines that life is like the bedtime stories I tell her: you can start over and over again, with the same pauses, the same intonations. You just have to insist. I try to explain that it's more complicated, that Amélie's parents may have other things to do besides walk to the ponds and, for that matter, so do we: we haven't finished moving in, we still have boxes to unpack, and while you can ask your father to reread the same story ten times, you can't necessarily assume that the entire universe must submit to your every wish, and … The phone rings, rescuing me from my predicament. Josée. Josée saying, you must be very busy unpacking and all that — why don't you bring the children to our place, we'll look after them for the day. No no, yes yes. In fact I wanted to paint the rec room, and her offer couldn't come at a better time. I make an agreement with Marie-France: I'll deliver the kids and come right back, okay? Okay.

Marie and Mathieu, who didn't stop their chatter and questions while we were crossing the park, treat me like a total stranger the minute we get to Josée's. As soon as Alex and Amélie come into their field of vision I cease to exist. Why strain your neck talking with grown-ups when there are kids whose eyes and ears are at the proper height? I don't exist any more, nor does Josée for that matter. Now we are both invisible and so we make coffee which we'll take outside and drink in the yard. On the garden table are some Prismacolor crayons and some colouring books that the children abandoned when we arrived. Josée proudly shows me the drawing she was working on: a magnificent full-length portrait of Albator, the space pirate. I congratulate her on her choice of colours and since I think I have a certain talent for colouring — I never go outside the lines — and I'm quite fond of Albator's spacecraft, I take my turn working on it.

The four children are playing in the house, and we're

highly responsible parents: constantly on the lookout, we worry at the slightest sound, and even more at the silences. But why shouldn't we also take some advantage of the pleasures of this July morning?

Colours, the arts, psychological tests, music and streams, school and the Virgin Mary: we have time to broach all these subjects and many more while we're wearing down our blue crayons — there's always too much sky in that kind of drawing. We're elsewhere, so much so that when Robert comes and joins us, we jump.

"Hope I'm not disturbing you."

He comes and sits with us, holding his coffee cup. Hard to imagine two worlds more different: Robert has worked hard on the late shift and he's still filled with night, with sleep and fatigue, while Josée and I have not only been awake for hours, we're colouring new skies.

"Sorry to disturb you..."

You have to know Robert to imagine the tone: though his eyes are half-shut and he is unshaven, his mind is always on the alert, so he'll come out with one of those remarks that you never know how to interpret. Always a little mocking, gently poking fun. And an expert at the art of making you feel guilty — goes with the job, I suppose. Or was I the one who was an expert, an expert at feeling guilty? Whatever the case, I feel a slight awkwardness that morning, a slight awkwardness that makes me gulp my coffee and go home, where I have walls to paint.

"Don't worry," Josée tells me. "No one will touch your drawing. I'll make sure."

So I go home and attend to my tasks, replacing the Prismacolor crayons with a roller that applies a single colour, perfectly uniform, to the rec room wall. And while I'm applying colour to the walls, I think about Josée, of course. About her smile, about how she seems to love colouring, about her tranquility ... I paint the walls of my house and never go outside the lines, but my mind is elsewhere.

When I go to pick up the children around five, Josée won't be there. Gone shopping. It's Robert, fully awake this time, who will offer me a beer that I'll feel obliged to accept.

And then I go home with the children, my head in the clouds a little, and a lot more disappointed than I'll admit to myself at not seeing Josée again, and at the same time upset at being so disappointed: what story are you cooking up for yourself, man? You've spoken to that woman for ten minutes max; how come you're thinking about her so much?

THE IDEAL STORY

few days later it's our turn to transform our house into a playschool. Fair enough. Robert, on his way to work, drops off the children. As soon as they're out of the car, Alex and Amélie disappear, as do Marie and Mathieu. If there's nothing more demanding than one child, four of them leave you absolutely free. The children cancel each other out, to quote Robert, who's an expert at finding the right turn of phrase.

The girls shut themselves away in Marie's bedroom, which has been transformed into the realm of the pony, and the boys putter around in the basement. They all get along so well, it would be criminal to keep them from seeing each other. Why would we want to stop them anyway? Even Mathieu, the least sociable, is transformed when he plays with Alex. They have the same tastes, the same way of moving, the same kind of imagination. It's pure pleasure to observe them run their Playmobil garage, so much so that Marie-France and I consider putting chairs in the rec room and spending the rest of the afternoon watching the boys play.

Around four o'clock Robert calls to say that he has to work late and won't be on time to pick up the kids. I offer to take them home instead: I spend all week cooped up in an office, I'd be glad to get some fresh air … I have no trouble persuading him.

I tell Marie-France and suggest that she come along: she could get some fresh air too, it would be fun to go together … I'd like her to agree, that way I wouldn't feel guilty, but I don't really mind when she refuses.

Persuading the kids, though, is another story: we just got here, it's unfair. And they whine and they stamp their feet …

Recalling the basic rules of negotiations, I give them the following choice: either I drive you home, which unfortunately will only take two minutes, or we walk, which will give you more time to play together … They fall into the trap of course and everybody's happy. Which goes to show that we do learn some useful things at university.

We walk through the park in a procession: the two girls in the lead, discussing the respective merits of braids versus ponytails; the two boys after them, talking about some movie that seems to feature a lot more explosions than dialogue; and finally me, bringing up the rear, and feeling more and more guilty at having manipulated everyone so deftly.

Josée greets us in her yard, all smiles, and offers me a glass of white wine, which I don't turn down.

We talk about the children, about how much they like playing together, about the diving lessons for which we'll have to sign the girls up next fall, about ponies and the action film that impressed the boys so much. It's at that very moment that Josée asks me point blank to tell her my ideal story.

"My ideal story?"

"You know, the movie you'd watch over and over, the novel you'd read again and again, without really knowing why…"

While I'm thinking it over, she tells me about Robert's fascination with stories about escapes: the prisoner of war who digs a tunnel with a spoon, who wears out his fingernails on stone, who doesn't even *have* fingers from digging night after night, for months and years. Secret courage, tenacity, solitude: those are the qualities Robert finds irresistible. He's seen *The Great Escape* ten times.

For Josée, nothing can beat the final scene in *Lassie*, when the dog runs through a forest, swims across an icy river, and finally, exhausted, leaps into the arms of Tommy, who thought she was dead. A dog and a little boy. Unwavering friendship, the absolute devotion of a pet, their love, which triumphs over all obstacles ... She goes wild over it every time. (And I too go wild that day over her story.)

As for me, I confess I've always had a weakness for "The Ugly Duckling" and all its variations. And I'm still very moved not by a story, but by a particular scene, one I probably recall from a war movie, but I'm not sure. I often think about the scene when I'm walking and amusing myself by composing scenarios. Let's suppose there's a soldier, fighting a war. A just war, of course, but one that's dirty too — a trench war, with mud and rain. A war you don't come home from, or if you do, you're horribly mutilated. Fifty times, a hundred times, the soldier gazes at a photo of his fiancée to revive his courage, to persuade himself that there exists on earth one place where life can be beautiful, where everything's not dirty and slimy and sad like the trenches where he's rotting away. But the war goes on for so long that the photo is worn thin from being folded and unfolded. The dampness eats away at it until finally, at the end of the first year, all that remains is a shapeless scrap of paper on which the soldier alone can still imagine the face of a young woman.

At the end of the second year, he doesn't even dare to unfold it, for fear it will disintegrate in his fingers.

When he finally comes home after three years, nothing is left of the photo, not even the smallest piece, the slightest shred: the war has soiled it completely, rotted it totally. If he had preserved a piece of that photo, a particle, a scrap, his fiancée would no doubt be there on the platform waiting for him. But he has lost the photo, lost the woman he loves: on the deserted platform, no one is waiting for him.

He gathers up his canvas bag, tosses it over his shoulder. And then, just as he's about to leave the station, he sees his fiancée, over there, at the end of the platform; he sees her running towards him, it's not a vision, it's not someone else, it's her, it's really her, throwing herself into his arms … Everyone thought he was dead, everyone but her. She knew that he'd come back, she never lost hope. They embrace with a sunset in the background, and superimposed on them are the words, THE END.

"Our stories are the same," says Josée. "The characters and events don't matter, it's the same theme: separation, pain, reconciliation … What about Marie-France?"

"Marie-France?"

"Her ideal story …"

"You'd have to ask her. I don't really know …"

"*You don't know?*"

She looks at me, frowning, stunned, incredulous even. As if it went without saying that everyone knows their spouse's ideal story. As if it were the first question you asked a girl after, What's your sign? Marie-France's ideal story? She's seen *Gone with the Wind* and *The Sound of Music* ten times, and she must have read *Jane Eyre* as often … I'm still trying to find the common denominator when Robert comes home from work.

"Hope I'm not disturbing you," he says, stepping into the backyard.

I tell him no, though I was thinking yes, and then we talked about the fascinating case of tax evasion he is investigating. I'm not being ironic, it really was fascinating, but I had trouble taking an interest.

THE TOURISTS ARE BORED

I see Josée often during the following weeks and months, but just a little at a time. And we're never alone.

I see her often but we barely have time to exchange two words: I'll drop Marie off with her and leave with Alexandre, or the reverse; she gives me some Kleenex to wipe a bleeding nose, I explain to her that Amélie's sweater got a little dirty because they were playing in the dead leaves and she'll have to be careful next time she washes it, there may be sand in the pockets, and chewing gum, and the beginning of a stone collection ... I help her tie Alexandre's boots and I repair Amélie's ponies' castle, while she teaches Mathieu how to tie laces so they stay tied, or scares Marie to get rid of her hiccups. You see the kind of situation I mean? Nothing to make a spouse jealous, and nothing to do with a porno film.

—

Imagine a huge picture and a painter who likes to confuse the viewer: first he paints a big suburban blue sky, then he adds a tiny spot of red, for a bleeding nose. After that, he goes to the other end of his canvas and paints a pony in fluorescent green, some remote-controlled cars, and hockey sweaters, bathing suits and white skates ... A few years later, with the benefit of hindsight, it will be obvious. For the time being though, no one can guess the painter's intentions: they're simply small pieces, scattered fragments, signs that accumulate and won't take on meaning till much later.

I remember a magical moment partway through the first autumn. A beautiful October day, with the caressing light that creeps in between the trees rather than crushing them. And leaves that have held the last rain, and the aroma of damp earth, and the mud puddles to avoid, and the boys who don't miss a single one ...

We're coming back from the pool. Alex and Mathieu walk in front, followed by Amélie and Marie, and finally the adults. Robert and Josée, with Marie-France and me bringing up the rear.

Josée is humming an old French song, which inspires her to make up a question game: she gives us a line, we have to guess the title of the song. *His car drives away without a sound; Spring's a lovely time to talk of love; A blind man plays the barrel organ.* You get ten seconds ... *The street lights up. Tell me, when will you return? One day, you'll see ...* Because I knew all the answers, it's my turn to suggest the lines.

"*Les moules et les frites, les frites et les moules …*"

"'Jef,' by Jacques Brel. That was too easy!"

"*The others all behind and him in front …*"

"'The Little Horse,' poem by Paul Fort, music by Georges Brassens."

"And I thought I knew French songs! I've met my match, I'm even outdone. *The tourists are bored in the back of their bus …*"

This time, I score a point.

"It's Charles Trenet, for sure," Josée replies, "but which one?"

She gives up, I provide the answer: "*Le jardin extraordinaire*," of course … She doesn't know Trenet all that well, it's her weak point, but she still knows by heart "*L'âme des poètes*," and "*Coin de rue*," and "*Il pleut dans ma chambre*," and soon we have to stop because we're the only ones playing the game.

Maybe I shouldn't have said I'd met my match. There's a sense of uneasiness.

PERFECTLY OBVIOUS

A little later, winter. The two of us are sitting in the stands at the municipal pool, where our daughters take diving lessons. We fill our lungs with chlorine, we touch each other's fingertips by accident while offering one another mints, and we make up new games, new journeys: first we go to Paris, "to every faubourg," we "climb the stairs of the Butte Montmartre which are hard on the poor," we "happen to cross the Pont des Arts," then we "fly to Brussels," where we "catch the thirty-three tram to go to Eugène's for frites." And then it's off to Amsterdam and Ostend, Göttingen and Marienbad, *Bruges et Gand* ...

We travel so far and we're so comfortable together that back in Longueuil we have a slight case of jet lag. Especially because Élisabeth, the diving instructor, takes us aside to tell us once again that *our* daughters are very talented.

Our daughters ... There's something magical between Josée and me, something obvious, so obvious that it's palpable. Someone has to see us together just once, at the rink or in the park and they'll assume right away that we're husband and wife. I don't know how many times I've been taken for the father of her children and she for the mother of mine, and people are always astounded: four children, that's so rare nowadays! Even when people do know, even when we explain the situation, they still make the mistake. It's as if life wanted us to meet before we even knew one another, wanted us to marry despite ourselves, as if the whole world wanted to throw us into one another's arms.

Something magical. Something obvious. Perfectly obvious. So much so that we had to wait for seven years before I dared to touch her shoulder with my lips.

Before that, there'd been just one temptation, one gesture. It happened at Place Longueuil. Hard to imagine a more idyllic place for a tête-à-tête, right? To make it even more romantic, picture the December 22 crowds: the pushing and shoving, the heat, the Christmas music — an unmitigated horror show. Enough to prompt you into bringing out the bazookas to destroy the universe, without a hint of remorse or fear of punishment: if God exists, I'm sure He understands. I'm at Sports Experts and I'm looking at cross-country skis for my kids — a plastic model for pre-beginners — when I feel a hand on my shoulder. I turn around: Josée, who's considering the same skis. Josée smiles at me and I forget the crowds, I forget the Christmas horror show.

There's an endless line at the check-out, but all at once I discover a wealth of patience: Josée is singing, "Boom, when your heart goes boom" to herself, and she's able to get me to hum the refrain. I look at her and I think she's beautiful. I look at her and I get one of those bursts of love that don't come often in a lifetime, though God knows there's nothing in the atmosphere to foster such a feeling. I set my skis on the counter, Josée does the same, and in the crush we realize, too late, that the cashier has written a single bill.

But we aren't going to ask her to redo her calculations: the line is getting longer and we're baking in our coats. I pay with my credit card, we'll sort it out later.

We decide to work out our finances in one of the fast food joints in the mall — fluorescent lighting, cardboard pizza, burgers cooked under electric lights. The atmosphere is once again outrageously romantic: it's hot, it smells of popcorn and damp wool, the coffee's disgusting and our ears are being battered by Christmas Muzak, but we talk and talk and soon we're all alone in the world. It's the first time, the very first time that she and I have been alone, just the two of us, with no kids. Sometimes we have to search for our words, sometimes they come in a rush; our sentences are awkward and often they limp along on one foot, but we don't need things spelled out, we don't need to draw pictures, and there's no one in this mall except the two of us. We talk about the cashier's error, then about all the others, errors relating to us, about all the people who surely couldn't be making the same mistake when they see us together, about all the errors mounting up, about all the people who after all couldn't be making the same error at the same time (could it be that thousands of errors end up creating the truth?), and as soon as we feel we've gone too far along that slippery slope, we move on to Robert and Marie-France, and we repeat to ourselves that we love them and that we certainly won't do *that* to them.

There's a silence and we start talking at the same time about errors and coincidences, about the signs that are mounting up, about what is perfectly obvious and is bringing us together, and once again the ground gives way beneath our feet. Marie-France and Robert don't deserve to have us do *that* to them, not to mention the fact that we've *already* hurt them, there are all those hints, those ellipses …

All our words say no, but our eyes say yes, so much so that I feel I have to do something, to say what can't be said, to prove to myself that I haven't made all this up, that I'm not dreaming. I put down my coffee, I put my hand on the table and, rather than keep it in my own territory, I inch it towards her, very slowly, so she'll have time to refuse; I move my hand towards her and I look her in the eyes so I can be quite certain that she understands what's happening to us, and I can feel my heart bursting through my chest, and I can see her move her hand towards mine, imperceptibly, see it come to meet mine, and finally our fingers touch, our hands brush each other for a second, just one little second that seems like forever, one little second and that's all: I hardly have time to feel its coolness, hardly time to feel the spark when she withdraws her hand and looks down, turning red. And then she raises her head and looks at me with blazing eyes, with smouldering eyes — forgive me the cliché, I can't come up with anything better.

And then we stammer something or other, we say that it's late, that in another life maybe, in another life *certainly*, that if only there were cracks in the space-time continuum … We say again that maybe in another life, but that we mustn't, it's impossible, we could hurt so many people so much, wreck so many lives; we repeat all that because we know it's required, but we don't believe a word: it is in this life, this life here and now, that we're saying all this and the looks we exchange are contradicting us as we speak.

Nothing happened, right? Nothing. It's a coincidence, life has played a trick on us, nothing happened, nothing … We allow some time to pass, we let things settle down, and what are we actually talking about? Nothing happened, absolutely nothing.

We finally tear ourselves away from our plastic seats and go our separate ways, forgetting all about the mix-up around skis and credit cards.

༈

So there I am, in my car, in the Place Longueuil parking lot. On the backseat, children's skis. I think about Marie and

Mathieu who are at home, expecting me. About my five-year-old daughter and my three-year-old son who are fed up with waiting for Christmas, about my daughter and my son who are expecting their father, who are expecting their father to be strong, sturdy and reliable, as upright as an oak tree ... Or that he be there, quite simply. That he be a father.

I think about Marie-France, to whom I've always told the truth, the whole truth, nothing but the truth. Marie-France, to whom I'll say nothing. Nothing happened, after all, absolutely nothing. The kind of nothing that turns your life upside down. The kind of nothing that I'll cling to for the next six years ...

An aggressive car horn shakes me out of my torpor: it's December 22, and here I am in my car, daydreaming like an idiot, and occupying a precious parking space while I'm at it. If I were in the United States I'd have been dead long ago. "I killed him because he was daydreaming in his car," explains the murderer to the judge, who dismisses him on the spot: how can anyone occupy a parking space in a mall to daydream on December 22? If that's not reckless behaviour, then it's sheer provocation.

And so I give up my space and drive home, not too sure how I'm able to drive at the right speed, to stop at the red lights, to switch on my turn signals: how does the body do it, know how to act when the brain and the heart are somewhere else?

THE ACCIDENT

*N*ormally, we would have let a few days go by, a few weeks even, and then we'd have seen one another again — life would have given us no choice in any case. We'd have exchanged furtive caresses, first with our eyes, then with our fingertips, we'd have allowed the tension to go up until it became unbearable, and then we'd have ended up in a motel on Taschereau Boulevard, or maybe even in a car, as good North Americans mindful of preserving traditions. Once, just once ... And then we'd have started again, again and again, because we wouldn't have been able to do otherwise, telling ourselves each time that what the others don't know can't really hurt them, and maybe we'd have called upon modern physics, which allows for the possibility of parallel worlds ... No need to go on: you know the scenario as well as I do, and you know what treasures of the imagination can be called on in such circumstances.

The others would have found out in the end, inevitably, because the situation would have become intolerable, because there's nothing more urgent for people in love than to proclaim it from the rooftops; lacking the courage to confess everything, we might have left some clues and hoped that the others would decide for us ...

That's how it would have happened. Normally. But some-times life is not normal. And has accidents in store for us. Terrible accidents even, that turn everything upside down.

ౘ

Amélie, all curls and ribbons, Amélie and her big blue eyes, Amélie brimming over with life, Amélie, who loves the water even more than Just Plain Marie, if that's possible. The kind of child you put in a pool for the first time and splish splash, she's at the other side, and then she does another ten lengths, on her stomach and on her back, and then she gets out and asks you when the lesson starts, when do I learn how to swim. You put her in the ocean at Gaspé, you show her where Europe is, and she's on her way, quite calmly, splish splash, with a smile on her lips. Incredible talent. But too much talent is dangerous: you fear nothing, you ignore danger. What exactly happened no one knows. A stumble? A momentary lapse in concentration?

Élisabeth, the instructor, is looking elsewhere. It's not her fault: she can't do everything, keep an eye on everything; besides, the lesson hasn't really started. Josée doesn't see anything either. She's sitting in the stands, by herself, her nose in a book.

No one sees Amélie climb onto the three-metre board and lose her footing on the last step. Did she hesitate, was she scared, did she want to turn back? She falls on her back, her head strikes the ground ...

It was the silence that pulled Josée out of her novel. The horrible silence that parents fear so much, the silence that screams in your ears that something terrible has just happened ... She looks up and sees her daughter, motionless on the ground, and Élisabeth and all the children around her, frozen, and time stops and nobody breathes.

The pool employees are models of efficiency: the head lifeguard saw what happened from his office window and has phoned the ambulance at once, while Élisabeth sees to it that Amélie isn't moved, that she's given air, that no one shouts at her. She speaks to her in her ear, very softly, tells her hang on, everything's going to be fine, she manages to find the right words and the right tone to tell her everything is fine, that she has to keep breathing, just go on breathing ... Soon Josée is at her side, adopting the same tone: everything's fine, Amélie, everything's all right, all you need to do is breathe, we'll take care of you ...

The ambulance drivers are just as efficient, as are the doctors at the Charles LeMoyne hospital, who immediately diagnose a cranial trauma and stabilize Amélie's condition before they transfer her to the Sainte-Justine children's hospital, where she will be in a coma for three weeks.

Three weeks. Three weeks of that terrible silence parents fear so much. Three weeks during which Josée and Robert take turns at their daughter's bedside, day and night. Three weeks of talking to her and not knowing if the words are making their way to her brain, if she can understand them, if she'll survive. Three weeks of stroking her forehead, her hair, and her hands, of cooling her face with a damp cloth, of helping the nurses treat her pneumonia — as if the concussion and the coma weren't enough, she has to get a lung infection too…

Three weeks of whispering words of love in her ear, many more words of love than most children will hear over the entire course of their lives. Three weeks of silence, and then, at last, she opens her eyes. Ten seconds or so at most. She opens her eyes on her father but doesn't recognize him. She goes back to her silence until the next day, when she opens her eyes again and recognizes her father, even gives him a hint of a smile before she goes to sleep. Yes, sleep: according to the doctors, it's not a coma now, but sleep. A sleep that seems restless and uneasy, as if she has to catch up with three weeks' worth of dreams — of nightmares, rather.

It will be at least another week before she is fully awake, and much longer before she can eat on her own, wash herself, walk. When she leaves Sainte-Justine, in a wheelchair, it will be to go to Marie-Enfant, where she will spend two months relearning all that. Josée and Robert will still be there, practically day and night, to show her how to use scissors or a hairbrush, how to turn the pages of a book, to make curls and braids. When she leaves Marie-Enfant, Amélie will be able to make braids for her ponies, but she'll still need to learn how to speak. Josée will take on most of her rehabilitation, with the help of a speech therapist. She'll need a full year of rehab before she can go back to school, where she'll need another year to make up for the time she has lost.

Today, Amélie is a lovely twenty-year-old medical student. Aside from some stiffness in her shoulder that prevents her from making certain movements, there isn't a trace of her accident.

That's why there's never been a motel or the backseat of a car, that's why there hasn't been a *normally*: there were other things to do that were much more important.

That's why for the next six years our love was banished far, far away, though it didn't disappear. It was elsewhere, if you wish. Dormant, rather.

And during all that time, threads continued to be woven together, lives continued to intersect.

OTHER THINGS TO DO

Other things to do, much more important. Talking to Marie, for instance. Explaining to her that sometimes life's like that, that a person can be a diving champion and make really gorgeous braids on her ponies and still have an accident, that it's unfair, that it can happen to anyone, any time, and maybe that's why we have to love life, and remind ourselves that time is often the best medicine and we have to trust it: time will heal Amélie, you'll see ...

One other thing to do, much more important. Starting the very next week, we go back to the pool. Josée, Robert, Marie-France, Élisabeth and I agree: it's the best attitude to adopt. Go back to the pool as quickly as possible to ward off bad luck, to clearly declare that life goes on.

And so there we are in the stands, Marie-France and I with Mathieu and Alexandre, who've never looked so serious. We watch Marie, little Just Plain Marie, my tiny little Marie, minuscule in her blue swimsuit, we watch Marie and all the other children in the diving class who are shivering and squirming while Élisabeth delivers a speech in which much is said about Amélie and her accident, about caution and bravery, about life, which goes on.

Marie breaks away from the group, walks up to Élisabeth and whispers something in her ear, then she goes directly to the three-metre board. Slowly, she climbs the ladder, without stopping at the place where Amélie stumbled and without ever looking down. When she gets to the board, she steps up decisively and jumps. It's not a dive, it's a jump, just a jump: feet together, arms close to her body, she lets herself drop, straight as a candle, and with eyes wide open. Her fall lasts forever, but the water is scarcely disturbed when she breaks through its surface. She lets herself descend into the blue water and the bubbles, lets herself sink deeply, without resisting, and comes back up immediately, as if shot from a cannon. When she finally bursts out of the water, she's displaying a big grin such as I've never seen on her, the big grin that she'll wear now after every dive, that will win over the judges every time: a grin of quiet triumph, determined and confident, that makes her look incredibly old for her age.

She swims to the edge of the pool while we stay rooted there, so impressed that we don't dare to applaud or even breathe — had we breathed while she was underwater, we'd most likely have drowned in our emotions. Maybe, too, we sense that Marie is in another world, and we don't want to wake her up.

Élisabeth holds out her hand and hauls her out of the water, then she whispers something in her ear, but Marie isn't listening — she has that look I know so well, the scowl that means she has no interest in what is being said or, rather, that she doesn't want to waste time on explanations: just let me do it, that will be a lot simpler.

Élisabeth speaks to her again, but Marie shakes her head, then she looks around as if she were trying to find Amélie. And then she goes back up on the board and jumps a second time, and a third, and a fourth, as if that could bring Amélie back, as if that could mend her. She jumps and jumps again, and each time she emerges from the water with the same quietly triumphant smile, and each time she is reborn.

Soon all the other children follow her and jump off the three-metre board, as straight as candles, and just as proud as Marie.

Élisabeth may have had other plans for the session, but she knows how to be adaptable. That Saturday there will be just one exercise on the programme: the candle-jump from the three-metre board.

THE GIANT WHO LIVES AT THE BOTTOM OF THE WATER

We all meet at the Sainte-Justine hospital that night. Gathered around Amélie who's unable to move, imprisoned by her cervical collar and tubes and wires, in her silence. Marie takes a seat in a chair beside the bed and starts talking to Amélie as if nothing were amiss. She describes each of her dives in the slightest detail: the bubbles, the chlorine, the way her eyes sting, the way her eardrums hurt; the fall, so quick, yet going on forever; and the push that you feel when you get to the bottom — it's as if there's a giant who doesn't want you to stay under the water, who boosts you up to the surface.

Marie never knew this, but Josée and Robert return to that story about the giant and repeat it to their daughter every day, with the same words, the same intonations —

the proper way to tell children a story: once upon a time there was a giant who didn't want little girls to stay in the deep water too long...

It's strange, the quirk shared by all children when they insist that we copy ourselves to perfection, repeat ourselves ad infinitum. They listen very seriously to whatever the story may be, brows furrowed as if they're aware that some crucial phenomenon is going on in their brains, that their synapses are being connected in a certain way, that circuits are being fixed forever. By asking to have the same stories repeated a hundred times, they are opening a path in the forest. They know that path will stay open even when the story is finished, and that they'll be able to follow it whenever they have problems. Perhaps hope is a muscle and the purpose of stories is to train it.

When she can speak again, Amélie will tell her parents that she often dreamed about a giant who lived at the bottom of the water.

WEAVING THREADS

*A*nother thing to do, much more important. Threads woven together, lives that intersect.

As Robert and Josée spend half their time at the hospital and still have to work as well, for a few months Alexandre becomes our third child.

We put him in a bed in Mathieu's room where he'll sleep every other night. When Amélie comes home and life gets back to normal, Alex will ask why he can't have two houses too, like all his friends at preschool. We'll have to explain to him, to Mathieu too for that matter, that two children aren't brothers just because they share a room, that they need to have the same parents too. They'll pretend to accept our explanations, but they'll never be entirely convinced.

It sometimes occurred to me when I went to tuck them in that Alex had seen much more of me than many children have seen of their own fathers.

ↄ

Threads woven together, lives that intersect. Since we often have to go to his house to fetch toys, pyjamas, or slippers, Robert gives me a copy of their house key. Whenever I have to use it, I'll go directly to Alexandre's room, without looking anywhere else, and I'll feel much guiltier than if I'd gone there to steal something.

ↄ

Threads woven together, lives that intersect. Robert has finished a hard day's work, he crossed the bridge at rush hour, he took Alexandre to a restaurant for supper, then stopped off at home to change, and now he's here at our door, worn out and haggard. He entrusts Alexandre to us before crossing the bridge again to join Josée at Sainte-Justine.

"Come on in for a minute, Robert. You could use a coffee …"

No way to make him sit in a chair in the living room: he'll gulp his coffee at the kitchen counter, and I'll see his hand shake, see the coffee spread over the counter.

"This doesn't make sense, Robert, you aren't going to drive in this condition … Leave your car here, I'll take you to the hospital. And if you want, I'll pick you up tomorrow morning."

He doesn't even have the strength to protest.

I'm sure you know the kind of conversation people sometimes have while driving in a car. Each person speaks to the vast night through which the headlights are hardly able to punch a hole; each person speaks to himself and at the same time to the car's other occupant ... Robert confides that he's never loved Josée as much as during these difficult days, that sometimes he doesn't have a shred of hope, only sorrow, but he just has to look at Josée, see the way she looks at Amélie, and he'll start to believe again ...

I don't say anything.

I walk with him to his little girl's hospital room, where Josée wants to spend another night, but Robert persuades her to go home, to sleep, he reiterates that wearing herself out won't accomplish anything.

Josée is sitting beside me, in my car. We are crossing the bridge, yet again.

"Tired?"

"Exhausted ..."

That will be the bulk of our conversation. We look out at the night, in which all the lights on the highways are hardly able to make a hole.

~

Threads woven together, lives that intersect. You can say without exaggeration that during these six months we form a single family. A big family. And Marie-France is thrilled:

there's always something to do, meals to fix, Alex's clothes to fetch, diving lessons, preschool, school, hospital, we're constantly on the run, and we love it, we're in our element. *Look for the busy guy*, as they say in management. The more we do, the better our organizational skills. The harder we work, the more time we have to get through a lot of work ...

Marie-France is terrifically efficient and very glad to be. She's radiant then, and all the more attractive. Maybe I'll have needed this accident to cure myself?

WAIT FOR MY JOY TO RETURN

WHEN DO WE LEAVE?

T walked a lot during the years when Amélie was learning how to speak again. Saint-Bruno or Saint-Hilaire, the Oka calvary or good old Mount Royal — there isn't a mountain in the Montreal region that I haven't climbed dozens of times, in every season, at every temperature, at every hour of the day, with a special predilection for Mount Saint-Bruno at dawn: the rise is so gentle that you're barely aware of it, and the winding paths always have in store new lakes, new perspectives, and sometimes a fleeting glance at a family of deer that are hardly even shocked to see us moving around in their pantry. You can walk for more than two hours without ever reaching the summit or the rocky peak from which you'd have a spectacular view, but the ever-changing landscape allows you to slowly debrief, to get rid of your

—

inner accountant till you can no longer add up two plus two, or even remember what "add" means.

But those are adult preoccupations. Whenever we want the children to come with us, Marie-France and I usually encounter a wall of indifference: walk with no destination, just walk, for no reason? Who wants to do that? To get us in shape? We already are. Admire the landscape? Get serious, papa: why would we want to look at lakes we can't swim in, trees we can't climb? And we've seen the summit of Mount Saint-Hilaire dozens of times … Mountains are for old people. We'd rather watch TV…

If they sometimes do tag along, out of spite or because they've got nothing better to do, we've no sooner started our ascent than the complaining begins: I'm tired, I want to ride on your shoulders, when can we go home, do we really have to climb the whole mountain?

If we want to walk to our heart's content we have to resort to cunning: first, I'll suggest an excursion to Saint-Hilaire, which results in the usual festival of pouts and lamentations; then, Marie-France will suggest, quietly, pretending it's just occurred to her, that maybe we could invite Alex and Amélie, I'm sure their parents wouldn't object, and …

Before she can finish her sentence the kids are in the car: when do we leave, what're we waiting for, can we climb three mountains today, just for a change?

"In any business, the power belongs to the person with the information," whispers Marie-France as she gets in the car.

"And his leadership — or hers — hinges on the way he lets that information circulate."

"You're making fun of us, we can tell," says Marie, who knows her parents and knows when they're up to something.

"We are not!" we reply in unison, though we can't hide the beginning of a smile.

When we were children, parents spoke English if they didn't want us to understand. Now they use the clichés of managers and academics: it's safer.

We stop at Robert and Josée's place and they greet us from their doorstep. Their faces are drawn, their smiles tired: thanks a million for taking care of Amélie, the fresh air will be good for her, maybe she'll finally be able to get the last of the hospital smells out of her lungs …

Their children are already dressed and they race between our feet to join Marie and Mathieu in the car, giving us hardly any time for the polite responses: don't mention it, you're doing us a favour by lending us your children, and if it will let you get some rest, then it's all to the good.

"Thanks again," Josée repeats, and I have the impression that these thanks are meant just for me. I bury them deep in my memory — I'll have plenty of time to decipher them — and reply with an embarrassed smile that I intend to convey something grave and important, but that probably looks more like an awkward scowl.

Back in the car, already full of the babble of four children, I turn the key and now I'm a father again. I drive slowly, stealing a look at Marie-France: she's admiring the scenery, pensive but smiling. A smile meant for no one in particular, not even for an idea or a memory. I know from experience that it's no use asking what's on her mind at moments like this. She is visiting a country of mist where time is drawn out, where words unravel, where she's comfortable, just comfortable, and she'd like to prolong this moment, mark it with a pause: Marie-France adores these family outings and if the family is growing, that's fine with her. She has admitted to me that she often dreams — only dreams — of having eight, ten, twelve children, and that every day is Sunday, and that we spend those Sundays climbing mountains. I try to drive smoothly so as not to draw her out of her daydreams, and I think about my father, who was a model of patience when his children were behaving like brats all the way to Uncle Léo's chalet: what could he be thinking about, what quiet thoughts was he entertaining to help him put up with our squabbling? He had the habit of saluting discreetly whenever he drove past a church. Now that it's my turn to drive, I'm the one who salutes; I salute him.

ॐ

No sooner have I parked than the kids bounce out of the car and start to run. Don't waste your breath suggesting that they conserve their energy, lay in supplies, or save anything at all: those are old people's ideas, papa. First we get tired out and then we rest. And why bother not overdoing it when there's no guarantee that we'll even get tired?

Luckily, the paths on Mount Saint-Hilaire start on a rather steep slope, which soon forces the children to adopt a pace that's suitable for everyone, and anyone with excess energy will soon come up with other ways to expend it: Alex and Mathieu are already looking for sticks they can use as both canes and swords, while the girls talk and talk and talk some more without ever feeling the need to catch their breath.

Amélie stops: a word that she should know has slipped her mind — something that still happens now, nearly a year after her accident. What she feels at such times is so strange that she has to stop walking and furrow her brow to come up with the recalcitrant word.

"What do you call it, the season when the leaves come off the trees?"

"Fall?"

"That's right, fall! Fall, fall, fall …"

She goes back to talking and walking, happy to have found that perfectly ordinary word, but a little further along, she stops again and asks Marie to show her something smooth: she isn't sure that she knows what that means.

Patient and understanding like a good teacher, Marie slides her finger along the trunk of an aspen while Amélie repeats the word *smooth* three times, as she usually does. Often she'll form three sentences that contain the new word, which, according to her speech therapist, should reactivate different areas of her brain: the trunk of the tree is smooth, smooth is a word that begins with an *s*, smooth as a skating rink...

The two girls quickly turn it into a game, so that Amélie by the time she reaches the top of the mountain, will have blithely relearned another ten or twelve words. Marie too, for that matter: she didn't know that the Richelieu River was named in honour of a man: Richelieu is a river, Richelieu is the name of a cardinal, and while a cardinal dresses in red, the river is always blue.

ॐ

It will take Amélie hundreds of hours of exercises, supervised by a therapist or by her parents, to regain her power of speech. When she came home after the accident, she'd forgotten the names of most objects, all verbs and their conjugations, and most numbers. Her parents bought her picture books and books to read, they showed her how to recognize cats and dogs, grapes and locomotives, and they told her stories about Christopher Columbus and Jacques Cartier, Louis Pasteur and Jesus. "It's as if we had the same child twice," they said, hastening to add that it wasn't a chore but a stroke of good fortune: the good fortune of spending time with her, of helping her, the good fortune of teaching a gifted child and learning along with her all those words and all those stories.

One year after the accident, Amélie can tell the difference between purple and ruby and grey and charcoal, but she no longer knows the meaning of the word *beige*. She can explain why leaves change colour and spell *chlorophyll* correctly, but she's forgotten the word *fall*. She knows that Richelieu was a cardinal, but she sometimes counts like a two-year-old: one, two, three, twelve, eight…

Years later, she still stops occasionally in mid-sentence to ask, somewhat dismayed: "What do you call that thing that's like a saucepan but with holes in it?"

She realizes that she ought to know the word, she can even picture the space it should occupy in her head, but every time, the sensation is just as strange: instead of the word, she can see only a blank space, like the faded areas left on a wall after burglars steal a painting. Every time, she'll feel robbed.

"A strainer?"

"Yes, that's right, a strainer … A strainer is a utensil, my brain is a strainer, I feel STRAINge …"

Amélie has learned her mother tongue twice, and while she now speaks it much better than most girls her age, she still often perceives it as a foreign language. It will have taken a lot of time and patience — not to mention a good dose of cheerfulness — to get back on her feet.

چم

—

No sooner have we reached the summit of Mount Saint-Hilaire than the children want to go back down. A box of raisins and some cartons of juice allow us to watch the Richelieu flow for another few moments, then we resume our walk to Lac Hertel, where we'll pause again.

"Frog babies are called tadpoles," says Marie. "Tadpoles don't look like poles, Mathieu and Alex are skinny like poles ..."

"And Marie's a dweeb," Mathieu retorts. "One dweeb, two dweebs, three dweebs ..."

Marie-France rebukes him gently, but Mathieu plugs his ears and runs away. Marie-France pretends to try catching him and I stay off to the side, happy to be witnessing these little family games. Then I'll take my time catching up with them: I like to stand off to one side and watch Marie-France walk. I like her ease, her suppleness, her hips like a little girl's: how can two children have emerged from there? It's a mystery ... and I'm moved once again by the contrast between her slender legs and her heavy hiking boots, her narrow shoulders and the huge backpack filled with provisions.

Finally I move closer to her, I take her hand, and I can feel her smiling all the way to her fingertips.

SHIFTING DREAMS

*F*or Marie-France and me these are happy years, when all our plans are realized with an ease that's almost indecent. We have good jobs that guarantee us the security we need, while allowing us to feel useful. We're able to use our brains without ever exhausting them. Our children are growing in grace and wisdom, with just enough illness and minor injuries to let us love them better. We have friends and family with whom we have harmonious relationships, with no quarrels or almost none. To show our gratitude to heaven, it would have to be Thanksgiving every Sunday.

Whenever we have disagreements, usually on household matters, we see them as opportunities for applying sound management practices: tell each other everything, negotiate everything. Zero inventory, zero loss, zero rancour.

First of all, let's present the problem clearly, with as little subjectivity as possible, and maintaining an open position.

"The house corresponds absolutely to my wishes, dear associate, with just one exception: there's no garage. Now, a garage allows its owner to park his automobile inside it and to accumulate tons of useless objects, but those virtues are merely incidental: a garage is first and foremost a building located judiciously at one end of a paved driveway, which makes it an ideal support for a basketball net. Since happiness without a basketball net is unimaginable, as a member of the masculine component of our enterprise, I suggest that we have a garage built."

"I feel your pain, dear associate, but have you considered that there's a way to get around any problem and that one form of happiness may be profitably replaced by another? Picture, if you will, a dog, on the lawn ..."

I should have seen it coming. As soon as the question arises as to what we lack in order to be happy, Marie-France responds with that business about a dog, and the discussion that follows is just as predictable: Mathieu and Marie-France want a dog, Marie and I prefer cats. To make everyone happy then, we'll buy a parrot, so be it ...

The dog's name is Cléo — Mathieu's idea, dug up who knows where — and the cat, Cléa. They enter the house on the same day, at the same time, and through the same door. Family harmony is too precious to risk damaging it with matters of seniority.

I pretend that my preference goes to Cléa, a calico female who's affectionate and playful, the kind of cat I like, but very quickly, and to my great surprise, it's Cléo who wins my affection. Like all golden retrievers, Cléo is a lovable and rather stupid dog, whose very stupidity makes him even more lovable: there's nothing funnier than watching him chase an invisible ball, come back empty-pawed, then start all over just a moment later, without ever getting tired. Although he's bulky and awkward, he's always very gentle with the children and even with Cléa. His coat is magnificent, and I have to agree with Marie-France that there's nothing like the beige of a golden retriever to set off the green of a suburban lawn, and vice versa. Besides, Cléo is always ready to go for a walk, always.

I enjoy walking along the paths of the extraordinary garden in the evening, not without some grumbling for form's sake.

Whether it's windy or raining or snowing, I let myself be tugged along by Cléo, who's liable to wrench my arm off whenever he flushes out a squirrel or a field mouse, or the remains of a sandwich or a chocolate bar. But when he's willing to let me think that I'm the master and gives me some respite, I can give myself over to my thoughts. And it never takes long before long they lead me to hum a Trenet song and think about Josée: her face appears in close-up at a bend in the road, and I feel myself melt, become liquid. I dissect her most recent words, I try to get back the substance of her last looks. I ask myself if her most trivial remarks concealed a hidden meaning or a secret message, and inevitably, I tell myself no, I was probably dreaming, I've got too much imagination.

Didn't I imagine that business of our hands touching at the mall? It seems so remote now, so strange that I wonder if it really happened or if it's not another of those dreams that come back abruptly at dawn, that seem so real we have to stop and think about them for a moment: those images that I saw so clearly — too clearly, maybe — were they *really* there?

I slow down — take it easy, Cléo, take it easy — I try to picture again those two hands brushing against each other, and I can't, I can't do it any more. The dream vanishes, and all that's left is Trenet's song: *Tonight the wind is knocking on my door ... Stolen kisses, faded bliss, shifting dreams ...* What comes next? Josée would know what comes next ... But she isn't here and that's that. It's to her daughter that she owes missing words.

And while my mind is idling as I think back on the event that may never have happened, there exists another story, all too real, that only needs a little goodwill to continue. A story about a family and a suburb, like in my most beautiful dreams. A story that has the most wonderful children, who sleep with their mother watching over them, in this house that Cléo could find with his eyes shut even if I kept him walking till tomorrow morning: that dog may be dumb, but he has flair. All right Cléo, we're going home. Maybe I'm cured, Cléo pal ... But one thing is certain, I've been had once again: for all that, I still don't have a basketball net.

THE INVISIBLE BALL

For our holidays we always choose inns or chalets with access to a lake or a pool; if we didn't, Marie would pack her bags and run away forever; but we also need a mountain to climb, or it wouldn't be a real holiday.

At Sutton or at Mont Albert, on the Appalachian Trail or at Mont Tremblant, there will always be an initial family excursion, generally disastrous: are we there yet, why do we always climb mountains, why do we *have* to take holidays?

"Because that's the fate of children, they have to pay their apportionment for family traditions ..."

I tend to make this kind of perplexing speech sometimes when I'm on the verge of exasperation.

"What's fate, papa?" asks Mathieu.

"It's an environmental tax," says Marie, who always pretends to know everything. "You're so stupid sometimes ..."

"You are too," replies Mathieu, understandably.

Then, turning to his mother: "Can we have our snack right now, mama?"

"But we've just left!"

"I know, let's pretend we're already there, then we can eat and after that we could go home ..."

"No way," Marie-France replies. "Okay, let's start walking!"

"Nice try," Marie will whisper to Mathieu a little later. "Maybe you aren't so stupid after all ... My turn now ... Mama, mama, my foot hurts!"

If they're in cahoots now on top of everything ... Tomorrow I'll take off by myself, with Cléo. He may be stupid but he never complains. Marie-France will stay in the chalet with the kids and I'll be able to walk to my heart's content. The day after, I'll take my turn looking after the children and Marie-France will have her day of freedom. And I'll suggest to the kids, let's clean up the cottage. Parents are entitled to take revenge now and then. I'll have them do so much housecleaning that they'll ask if we can go walking ...

"Look, papa," says Mathieu a little later, "I think Cléo's got a sore paw ... Maybe we ought to go home ..."

"Don't be silly; even if Cléo had four broken legs he'd still walk. *He* isn't a wimp ..."

And now Mathieu frowns and I regret wounding his pride. Why do I behave like that with him and never with his sister? Why is it that once we're parents we never have enough time to think *before* we speak? The worst thing is that Mathieu actually enjoys mountain walks. But since he loves his sister even more and he'd do anything to make her say that he's not so stupid after all ...

"Sore paw, Cléo? Wait, let's have a look ..."

I throw him an invisible ball and Cléo runs to the swamp, saunters through the mud, swims in the sludge. There's something touching about an animal that's so idiotic. Maybe I haven't been able to remove the thorn that I planted in Mathieu's heart, but at least I took his mind off it: now he throws the invisible ball at Cléo, who once again dives into the swamp.

"Why don't we go home right away, papa?" Marie will say as soon as Cléo has shaken off the mud. "Look, I'm all dirty and I think I felt a drop of rain ..."

"A little rain never hurt anyone. We aren't made of chocolate ..."

We aren't made of chocolate ... Another one of those parental remarks that comes straight from our own childhood, that we spout without thinking. Is there anything as depressing as opening your mouth and hearing your parents? As if, along with their genes, they had to pass on their clichés ...

"Okay, you win, let's go home."

ↄ

The next morning I set off at dawn with good old Cléo. So I can finally walk at my own pace and stay at Round Top as long as I want to admire the view. And to change the way I think a little, the way people do at the summit of a mountain. It often seems as if the thoughts that come to us there have a special quality, that they're more wholesome, more penetrating, more profound. For a long time I thought that was why colleges and universities were built on hills, until an economist pointed out that the land there was less fertile and therefore cheaper. Maybe it's because the effort we've expended to reach the summit makes those ideas more precious; maybe too the quality of the air makes us more appreciative of the most trivial reflections, who knows, but I do remember the sequence of my thoughts that day as I was climbing Mont Sutton.

First of all, I thought about John Lennon, and I tried to remember the words to "In My Life," without success. Still, I hummed the melody all along the way, mixing my own words with Lennon's.

After that, I thought about my father and his crazy dream of walking to the Arctic Ocean. It was a wacky notion that he'd often bring up when he was at Uncle Léo's chalet: he'd say that if he walked due north and never veered off, he could cross the Mont Tremblant park, then hike through the lakes and forests, the ice and tundra, for two thousand miles, that he'd meet foxes and polar bears, deer and caribou, but would never see even a shadow of a human being. Needless to say, he never took the first step on that strange journey, but he liked to dream about it. My father was a tireless dreamer who was able to revive the same dreams year after year; though he sometimes explored new paths, he always found his way. Too bad he wasn't able to do more walking.

I took other memories out of their drawers, studied them carefully, then filed them away in different drawers, for a change, hoping they'd still be able to astonish me the next time I uncovered them. And then I thought about my calves and thighs, which I could feel hardening, and I told myself you have to be a little crazy to do so much walking. Or be very old and have tons of memories to sort out. Or else be a refugee hunted down by an army of fanatics. Or, of course, be in love. The delayed-action kind of lover…

I thought about Josée, about life, which is always improvising, which doesn't know how to do otherwise. That there are errors and blunders is unavoidable. For one successful love story, how many others start up again and again, and always bump into the same obstacles? How many are abandoned along the way, after a promising start? Why get attached to something that may have been just a rough draft? There may be a masterpiece under the deletions, but I'll never know. The inks have run together for too long now. If I erased them I'd just tear the paper.

Since I was going around in circles, I finally allowed myself to go back to the framework of my ideal story, adding a few episodes: after landing in Normandy, where he has miraculously survived the sustained German gunfire, my soldier crosses fields and rivers, liberates towns and villages, then is wounded and takes refuge on a farm. (While he's there he will gaze at his fiancée's photo all he wants, while he waits for his fever to drop.) And then he gets back on the road, crosses the Rhine, wipes out the enemy's last factories, frees the prisoners, destroys the concentration camps, then walks, seething with rage, and enters Berlin, where he tracks down Hitler and drives him out of his bunker, hands in the air, and offers him up to liberated humanity.

And it's then, just as I'm sticking the tip of my bayonet into Hitler's back to spur him as far as the summit of Mont Sutton, that I realize I've made a mistake: the ideal story isn't the one about the simple foot soldier who ferrets out Hitler, any more than it's the story of the soldier who goes home to be with his fiancée. The ideal story is the story of all parents whose children are sick or handicapped or simply sad, and who care for them and console them and love them.

Hitler has vanished. Gone back to his bunker for good. Now, at the summit of the mountain, there's only Cléo, who wants to go back down and is seething with impatience, and me, gazing out at the landscape and wondering how I could have made such a big mistake, and over the course of so many years.

And all of a sudden I miss my children. I wish they were here, I wish I were listening to their complaining. Tonight we'll play Monopoly, I promise. A long game, and I'll see to it that I lose. And we'll stuff ourselves with ice cream and we'll go to bed when I want, I promise.

I pick up my bag and my stick and leave behind my rifle, my grenades, my ammunition: I'm no longer a soldier, I'm going home. Mission accomplished, Captain. But I still spare a thought for Josée as I look out at the landscape one last time: why is she the one I always think about, the one to whom I'd like to tell my story?

ON THE ICE

It was Robert who had the idea, nearly two years after the accident. No doubt he felt guilty at having neglected his son (if you're looking for excuses for feeding your guilt, I strongly recommend the parenting profession); but then again, perhaps he'd have made that decision in any case, I can't say; what I can tell you though is that he turned up at the house one Saturday morning, all excited, to announce his plan: our boys are six years old, they can skate — or at least they can stand up on skates — it's high time they went into hockey.

"Hockey? Maybe, but ... Come on in, let's talk it over. How about a coffee?"

No sooner have I finished my sentence than he's sitting in the kitchen, bombarding me with information he reels off: it costs this amount, they'll need that equipment, registration is at such-and-such a place, the season gets underway in two weeks …

I've never seen Robert so worked up, so much so that I wonder if he's still in the economic crime division, where his most thrilling activity is tracking down phoney receipts.

"Have your colleagues in narcotics made a big seizure recently? I could swear you've been shooting up pure adrenalin …"

But he's not listening, he's all wrapped up in his plan.

"See, the only problem is, there's a shortage of coaches. So I thought you and I could take on a team …"

"They form teams already, at that age? I thought they'd just learn how to skate …"

"Sure, they have to be able to skate, and hold a stick, but it goes quickly, you'll see: with two hours of coaching a week I bet they'll be playing games by December — just for fun, of course … How about it?"

"Hang on a minute, Robert. I've hardly had time to get used to the idea of my son playing hockey and you're asking me to be a coach … Me and hockey, you know … And our kids are only six, that seems a bit young to me … You want sugar for your coffee?"

"Just think about it: Mathieu rushes up with the puck, he passes to Alex …"

I ask him for a week to think it over, and that very afternoon I'm at Sports Experts buying sticks and skates, cups and elbow pads. It was a good idea, really. A very good idea.

A terrific adventure that will last till Robert and Josée decide to move to Quebec City.

On skates, Robert becomes a child again, only better: imagine a man who has only held on to the happy aspects of childhood. Just as Amélie and Marie are in their element when they swim, Robert just has to jump onto the ice and he's transformed into a kind of mutant who no longer knows how to walk and run, but who flies, soars, spins and then hits the brakes, spattering you with chips of ice — all this while fooling us with astounding magic tricks: see this puck? Whoops — it's gone! There it is, behind you …

The boys learn how to skate without even realizing it as they try to catch up to him, probably thinking they just have to take the puck from him and some of his happiness will rub off, and Robert has a knack for allowing them to catch up without letting it show too much.

Robert is the teacher, the inspirer, the chief, and I'm the manager: reserving ice-time, negotiating for tournaments, signing contracts (that's right, they make children sign contracts) — I look after all of that, as well as fitting on helmets and elbow pads, nursing aches and sparing egos, not to mention updating team statistics, always as flawless as ledgers. (So neat and tidy they look fishy, Robert tells me. You're sure you don't cheat just a bit when you calculate the average effectiveness of the goalie?)

A good idea, really. I don't know how many times I've thought about our team at work, even during important meetings: maybe we could have Jean-Sebastien play right wing, even though it would weaken our second line. How can we persuade Mathieu to free his zone as fast as he can without trying to outsmart everybody? I'll have to talk about it with Robert ...

~

I'm often at Robert's place on Sunday mornings, to work out coaching schedules: five minutes of intensive skating, then passing practice, after that two-on-one raids ...

While we draw up our plans, as serious as generals, Josée and Amélie, next to us, are reviewing their multiplication tables: four sevens are twenty-eight; four eights are thirty-two; four nines are ... are ...

"Another number that the thieves stole," says Robert. "Makes you wonder what fence took delivery of that thirty-six ..."

"Thirty-six!" exclaims Amélie. "Four nines are thirty-six; thirty-six; thirty-six ..."

And repeats *thirty-six* several times, to imprint it on her brain, while Josée looks at Robert with fake exasperation.

"That's cheating, Robert. No prompting allowed."

"Me, cheat? I was thinking out loud, that's all."

Four tens are forty; four elevens, forty-four; maybe we could put Jean-Sebastien on left wing; four twelves are forty-eight; we'll have to call Philippe, he missed practice again — he should be at his father's this week … Five ones are five; fives twos are ten … Shall I make coffee?

Threads that are woven together, lives that intersect. While Robert gets up to make coffee, I look at Josée, who is giving her daughter sheets of paper for working on her divisions. The paper is white, Josée's fingernails blood red …

"It was Amélie's idea," she explains before I say a thing. "She thinks it's pretty … What about you?"

I tell her it's very pretty, of course, though I'm thinking the opposite, and feeling uncomfortable at being caught: I must have been looking at her hand for too long and she noticed … Because of the red too: she has never used nail polish, never, I'd stake my life on it.

She hides her hands self-consciously when Robert pours her coffee.

჻

Josée sometimes comes to the matches with Amélie. No matter what the score is, no matter what the situation, she seems calm, relaxed, smiling. I sometimes look in her direction when her son has blocked a pass or if an opponent has outsmarted him: she seems to be the only one who remains impassive, the only one who hasn't succumbed to collective hysteria. To have such control over her emotions, she must be made of different stuff from ordinary spectators, or practise meditation under the greatest Zen masters, or …

"There's a more plausible hypothesis," Robert tells me. "Josée doesn't know a thing about hockey. The other day she asked me why Alex wasn't skating back and forth like the others, why he always stays at one end. I had to explain that her son was the goalie..."

I also told myself... A person can't be so impassive when her son is at war and dozens of enemies want to annihilate him, under the hostile shouts of parents howling insane remarks. When I feel battered by nervousness, at the most crucial moments of the game I look for Josée in the stands and very quickly spot her, no matter where she is: she's the only one who always has her nose in a novel.

As for Marie-France, she's incapable of coming to a game. Whenever she does, she's afraid she'll leave great slabs of her mental health behind. How can you sit for an hour on an ice-cold bench, totally helpless, your heart going two hundred beats a minute, watching your son get hammered? She can't do it, any more than she can attend Marie's diving competitions. The parents of divers may have a slightly thicker coating of civilization, which forbids them to shout terrible things, but that doesn't change the essentials: whether it's for Mathieu or Marie, Marie-France is afraid of fainting or even forgetting to breathe. She can't bear competition so she's decided she'll just come to practices. On days when there are games or competitions, she stays home.

I understand her: I couldn't bear to stay in my seat when Mathieu is playing; I much prefer my role of assistant coach, which lets me do my pacing behind the bench. When Marie dives, though, I don't have that expedient, and every time I'm afraid my ribs will break from the pressure of my heartbeats. For parents, all sports are violent.

I go to all of Mathieu's matches and all of Marie's competitions, trying not to let anything show, and I think I'm fairly successful, most of the time anyway. When Marie-France tells me that she can't understand how I can take so much pressure, I shrug nonchalantly: I like her to think that I'm strong.

NORMAL LIFE

*R*ibbons and scissors, tree and lights, and a big table on which Marie and Amélie are arranging red napkins that they fold into strange shapes; since they've been learning origami they can't walk past a sheet of paper without turning it into a frog or a unicorn. "Unicorn, unicorn, unicorn," repeats Amélie, closing her eyes, even though it's a word she knows well; she loves unicorns, she explains, and she wants to have one in her mind all the time.

"That's a good idea," says Josée. "There are all kinds of words that we should repeat to ourselves ..."

"Repeat, repeat, repeat," Mathieu pipes up. "If you say something three times is it three-peating?"

Three years after the accident, Amélie has practically no memory lapses and she can name everything in the dining room — chairs and plates, salt-shaker and wine glasses, corkscrew and olives. While she has recovered nearly all the words, she'll still repeat them three times, out of habit, and she doesn't seem to tire of naming whatever Marie points out to her: fork, knife, spoon, tablecloth, nerd …

"Nerd yourself!" replies Alex. "Amélie's a nerd, Marie's a nerd, that makes two nerds."

"Cut it out, children," says Josée, a hint of exasperation in her voice. "Can't you declare a truce? It's Christmas …"

"She started it," replies Alex, who doesn't skip a single childhood cliché.

"That doesn't mean you have to keep it up," replies his mother, who's also familiar with all the classic lines.

"I don't keep it up, she does! She always says everything three times! She keeps it up before I do!" says Alex finally, which stops the conversation for good.

She keeps it up before I do … Even after millennia of parenthood, certain children can still come up with lines that aren't automatic platitudes. Which goes to show that we should never give up on the future of humankind.

Josée shrugs and accepts with a smile the glass that Robert hands her. While the kids continue to exchange sweet nothings, the adults try to make themselves feel more comfortable by drinking wine — not at the dining room table, which is set for Christmas dinner, but at the kitchen counter, where they're perched on stools.

"Thanks for celebrating Christmas with us," Robert tells us softly. "It's largely thanks to you that …"

He looks at his daughter and his voice breaks. He coughs, embarrassed.

"Sorry, we don't often whisper a toast … So, I was saying, it's largely thanks to you that …"

Again he looks at Amélie, whom we can hear teasing Alex, and again his voice breaks. To help him out I say the first thing that pops into my mind.

"That we've nearly wiped out the Saint-Lambert Kings …"

"That we've nearly wiped out the Kings, right, and that we've nearly wiped out Amélie's memory lapses. Considering all the words she comes up with to aggravate her brother, I'd say that she's totally cured. I can't imagine a more wonderful Christmas and I can't imagine it except with you."

Definitely, there are reasons to celebrate: for a while now Amélie has recovered most of her vocabulary, and she's made enough progress in math to resume the normal course of her studies, if you can apply that word to a nine-year-old. After the Christmas holidays, she'll be in grade four, in the same class as Marie. She'll still go to a speech therapist for a while, but as for the rest she'll be back to a normal life. Her mother too, for that matter: since the accident Josée has only been working two days a week, in one school. Now that Amélie no longer needs a private tutor, she'll go back to her forty-hour week, her two schools, and her full salary.

"Glad to be living a normal life, Josée?"

"I could have done it for another year, to tell you the truth; but I wasn't going to tell my daughter to un-learn everything again … I … I don't know what to say, it's silly: now that Amélie is talking, we're the ones who have trouble finding words … Thank you for being here."

We raise our glasses and drink in silence, still a little uncomfortable at being there in spite of everything we have in common. This is the first time the four of us have been together since the accident, and it scares me: I've learned how to control the way Josée affects me, but only if I have just small doses of her. But a whole dinner at her side, looking at her, brushing against her, plus the effects of the wine … Ever since she and Robert invited us, I've been telling myself that story's over, that story never even got started; and it's Christmas, a holiday for children, we aren't important, at least we shouldn't be …

But counting on the children's presence to take my mind off Josée was obviously an error: they live in their own world and for them, we don't exist. Now there are just Marie-France and Marc-André, Robert and Josée — four adults feeling a little too present, who would be happy to exist a little less.

We try to appear relaxed, but we're stressed, we're stiff when we should be laughing, as if this were some dull social event and not a meal with friends. It may have something to do with our clothes: most of the time I've only seen Robert in jeans or sweats, or in his old torn Chicago Black Hawks sweater. Tonight the crease in his pants seems too sharp, and it's as if he doesn't dare move his neck for fear that he's left a pin in the collar of his new shirt.

Marie-France is also too dressed-up. While I'm used to seeing her dressed soberly, expensively and tastefully, I'm even more used to seeing her undress the minute she gets home to change into jeans and a T-shirt like everybody else, at the same time removing the invisible armour that keeps her from moving the way she moves when she's relaxed. Her movements then are so fluid that she glides through space like a diver making a perfect entry into the water, without splashing. This evening she hasn't removed either of her two suits of armour. In her black skirt, spotless blouse, and jacket it seems to me that she's performing, working. She didn't want to come here and it shows. She didn't want to come here and she hasn't. I watch her move when she goes to the table and unfolds her napkin to spread over her lap, and I sense that she's not there, even though her face is all smiles. She knows how to fool people, how to play on her charm, and above all how to use the smile that she can turn on at will and wear for hours, with no apparent effort. She didn't want to come here but she didn't dare say so: how could she turn down Robert's invitation to celebrate, together, their return to normal life?

Josée is wearing pants, as usual — I've never seen her in anything else — and a loose sweater in autumnal tones. She is partial to earthy and faded colours, dead leaves and oats, hazy, indefinable colours that stand out against the frankness of her face. Those colours suit her so well that I wonder if they're carefully chosen, if she had her colours done, but I can't imagine her paying for such a thing. Maybe they're simply her personal taste, and that makes it even worse; maybe, too, it has nothing to do with colours, maybe I'm attracted to everything about her and I've fallen into the trap, yet again: looking at her a little is already too much. Just as I'm trying to avert my gaze, she gets up to serve and I allow myself to admire her waist unperturbed, like that of Trenet's Madelon, and her sturdy hips ... By the way, in which song does Brassens talk about *sturdy hips*? Josée would know, of course, and she'd hum the chorus with me: "All is well where she is, not a thing to dispense with/When your isle is a desert, all you've got you've come hence with." But I don't dare ask her.

What were you saying, Robert? Sorry, I must have been daydreaming.

༈

The children gobbled their meal and left the table long ago. Now they're playing Nintendo while their parents persist in their inexplicable adult behaviour: they pick at bread and cheese though they're no longer hungry, they drink though they aren't thirsty, and they talk, they talk and talk as if it were an activity that called for sitting in one place without moving for hours.

They are speaking in an undertone (or so they think, but when you've had some wine it's hard to control the volume) about some of the great joys and about a few of the drawbacks to being parents, and their conversation is moving ahead briskly, at least until Robert loses the thread of his ideas when Marie-France takes off her jacket and drapes it over the back of her chair. As she didn't stand up during the operation, she made a very pretty movement that caused her breasts to stand out and emphasized her curves ... You were saying, Robert? Yes, the wine is delicious. Shall we go to the living room and distribute the presents?

❧

As soon as the children have unwrapped their new Nintendo cassettes and their remote-controlled cars, their comic books and their supplies of beads to string, they go back to their own world and continue to ignore us loftily: they have no desire to pretend that they're interested in the gifts the adults generally exchange, those boring things that they buy pre-wrapped and can't even play with, those useless knick-knacks that will soon be at the back of some cupboard ...

But they're wrong. That day, the adults' gifts reveal some surprises. While both Josée and Marie-France have received a silk scarf and bath oil, they've also been given some fat novels by John Irving and Margaret Atwood, novels they were so eager to read that they've found it hard to resist the temptation to dive in right away. Children aren't the only ones who can create a world for themselves and take refuge there at will.

Robert's surprise was unfeigned when he unwrapped the Bobby Hull hockey card, his childhood idol, that had cost me a small fortune in a store specializing in such mementoes. Then I had to suffer his sarcasm when I unwrapped the blade-protectors he'd offered me: now I won't be able to plead dull blades to explain my mediocre performance as a skater.

And after that I was thoroughly amazed to receive from Josée a recording by Jean-Roger Caussimon. While all the women of my generation worship Jacques Brel and some even manage like Léo Ferré, very rare are those who know Caussimon, with whom Ferré composed "*Monsieur William*," and "*Nous deux*," and "*Comme à Ostende*," and …

Maybe I could have contained myself and not shown my emotion when I unwrapped that disc. Maybe I should have played down my enthusiasm, maybe I shouldn't have sung "*Nous deux*" in a duet with Josée, maybe too I should have pretended to forget the words to "*L'écharpe*" and not sung along with her about *the memory of silk with its memories of you*.

༄

A silk scarf, a simple silk scarf. And I thought it would be the most banal present, the most indifferent, the least compromising, I told you about it, Marie-France, remember, we were together when we bought that scarf, I asked your opinion, you said it was a good idea, surely you don't think …

"What's going on with you two?"

"Nothing, absolutely nothing, I swear on the heads of our children there's nothing going on!"

We're back home now, but our thoughts are still at Josée and Robert's. We're in the living room, speaking softly over one last drink, as we always do on Christmas. Marie-France has taken off her uniform and got into a nightgown, she's taken off her armour too, as well as her smile. Sitting on the sofa with her legs folded under her, she's talking to me without looking at me, staring at the ice-cubes as she slowly swirls them in her glass. There's nothing aggressive in her voice, just curiosity, and a touch of weariness.

"What's that business about a silk scarf?"

"It's a song by Maurice Fanon, that was picked up by Félix Leclerc … A song that Josée knows. Just a coincidence."

"And was it a coincidence that the two of you spent all night looking at each other?"

"Look, we sang two songs together, not even the whole way through. That's six minutes out of an evening that lasted six hours. If there'd been an outside observer tonight, he'd have calculated that I spent 37.5 percent of the evening talking with Robert, 22.8 percent with the kids, 17.5 with you, 12.8 with everyone together, and let's see … 11.5 of the time with Josée. I apologize if that doesn't add up but I didn't have a stopwatch or a calculator. True, we sang two songs together. So?"

"You know perfectly well, it isn't about quantity. It's always the same thing: as soon as you two are in the same room it's as if the rest of the world doesn't exist. Just the two of you, in your bubble ... As if every sentence, every word, alluded to something, as if you'd known each other *before* ...

"Before what?"

"Before you met me, before Josée met Robert ... I don't know how to put it ... It's as if you can't stop yourself from looking at her, as if you're looking at her even when you aren't ..."

No point denying it, that would be ridiculous. What could I say? That I spent the evening trying not to look at her? That would be worse ... The truth, Marc-André? You have an obligation to tell her the truth, nothing but the truth, which is, as it happens, your best defence.

"The truth is, I find her attractive, I'd be a total liar if I denied it. Why? I don't know. If I knew, I wouldn't be so attracted. Everything you said is true: the complicity between us is so obvious that I also feel as if I've known her forever. True, I look at her even when I'm not looking at her. And it's true that if I were in another life I'd certainly see what it was about. But I'm not living two lives, I'm living one, and it's with you, with the children, and it's the same for Josée as far as I know: she doesn't seem particularly unhappy with Robert ..."

Marie-France believes me, I think: she finishes her drink, puts the glass in the dishwasher immediately, then comes back to the living room to sit and talk about the children, about their presents, about what makes them happy, about their minor disappointments too, which they haven't yet learned how to hide. It's not always easy to find the right things for them, to guess their wishes, but all things considered, we gave them a fine Christmas.

Very fine Christmases, which in future years we celebrate alone, just the four of us. As a nuclear family, to quote the sociologists. (What could he have been thinking about, the person who first put those two words together? Does a family have that much potential for violence?) If Robert and Josée insist on repeating the experiment (which would be surprising), we'll refuse politely, that's all. Not talk about it again, and go back as quickly as possible to the status quo: we'll be good neighbours and we'll exchange services, nothing more.

When we're getting into bed we've reconciled almost completely and we say nothing more about Josée or Robert, at least not till Marie-France says to me, in the dark: "It has to happen, one day or another..."

"No it doesn't..."

I replied very quickly, mechanically, stupidly, without realizing at the time what a terrible confession my unconscious had just delivered: I knew right away what that *it* referred to, and that I'd been wanting it forever.

THE YUKON, ROUND TRIP

*F*or anyone who's looking for solitude, a change of scene and wide-open spaces, there's something simpler and cheaper than the Yukon: there's nothing more strangely deserted than the streets of Longueuil on the morning of December 25. I'm talking about very early, the chilly dawn, when families are still asleep, dreaming of their presents, when people on their own are asleep without dreaming, having taken their sleeping pills. It's Cléo and his temperamental bladder that have introduced me to these vast zones of solitude, and I almost thank him for it.

The lives of dogs are really quite easy: they just have to moan softly, their head at ten minutes to twelve, to get whatever they want from you — especially if they go to the trouble of shaping one eyebrow into a circumflex accent. You can't really hold it against them to have wakened you, especially because reason quickly takes over from feelings; a walk in the fresh air costs a lot less than a rug cleaning; good dog, Cléo, we're on our way, just let me get dressed …

Yukon, six a.m. As soon as he's outside, Cléo rushes at the first tree and makes a deep yellow cave in the snow. You can see that I'm thrilled, Cléo, but if you think that the only reason I got dressed in boots and coat was to witness that sight, you're mistaken: an extraordinary garden on Christmas morning must be extraordinary to the power of two, right? It's minus twenty, the sun will be up soon, imagine walking in the snow, the freshly fallen snow, without those big chunks of salt and crushed gravel that get stuck between the pads of your paws … I could even let you run without your leash, Cléo pal: I don't think the police are out at this time of day.

Walking in the snow, in the heart of the Yukon, and talking together, sotto voce, then talking to myself. *It has to happen, one day or another* … I thought about it all night, old Cléo, all night thinking about *it*, which I can imagine all too easily; I thought it over all night and I still don't understand how Marie-France could make such a prophesy. Does she hope, even unconsciously, that it will happen? And as long as we're playing fifty-cent-an-hour shrink, is it not in my interest for Marie-France to be unconsciously hoping for it? Do you follow me Cléo? This is what's called going around in circles in the heart of the Yukon, isn't it?

The less I see Josée, the more I feel as if I've known her forever, and the more I feel that Marie-France, whom I *have* known forever, is a stranger to me. What good is it to keep from seeing Josée? I'm going around in circles in any case. Maybe I should stop trying to avoid her. Maybe I should, on the contrary, try to trivialize the situation. Do you think that makes sense, what I just said, or is it my desire dressed up differently? Whenever I reason that way, I have the sense that I'm seeing a chasm opening before me, the kind of chasm that my father tried, in vain, to fill with alcohol. My own tendency is to walk. And when I'm cold the way you can be cold in the heart of the Yukon, I just walk a little faster, that's all.

Let's suppose that it does happen. Let's suppose. Since I already feel guilty, I may as well feel guilty for a reason, right? But how to go about it, how to tell her? Even when I was young and single I was never very good in situations like that.

At magical thinking, though, I was a champ. Let's suppose that Josée has got up early too, even if she doesn't have a dog to waken her. She's got up early just like that, for no particular reason, she wraps her neck in *the memory of silk with its memories of you*, then she feels like going for a walk in the extraordinary garden, to take advantage of the Christmas sales on trips to the Yukon. "The Yukon at your door," to quote the slogan in the travel agency window. Continue straight ahead, turn left, there you are. And it's free …

She's walking, happy, and she appears, there, right there, where the path turns after the grove of fir trees. She appears there, right there, and we're so amazed at meeting, so dazzled by the obscure power that has driven us towards one another, that we don't have anything to say. We touch fingertips, then lips, and we close our eyes, and at once, a climate shift transforms this snowy park into a Caribbean beach; there's even — why not? — a straw hut, a straw hut with a switch at the door to stop time ...

And then I wake up, I look at the roof of the hut and I picture Marie and Mathieu who've stayed behind, in Longueuil, who are asking their mother: "Where's papa?"

And Josée looks at the thatched roof too, and she thinks about Alex and Amélie who've stayed behind, in Longueuil, who are asking their father: "Where's mama? She wouldn't leave us on Christmas, would she?"

"It's nothing," Marie-France and Robert reply. "An attack of irresponsibility, that's all. These things happen, it's because of their age. They'll be back tomorrow, it's nothing ..."

Yes, they'll be back tomorrow. And all they'll have managed to do is to make their loved ones suffer.

The magical thinking breaks down. It seems to me it was a lot more independent when I was young. A drop of fuel and I was off for weeks. I don't know about dogs, but for us humans, getting old must be something like that: our walks are longer, but our dreams are shorter.

I don't understand everything, old Cléo. I do my best, but since I'm not alone it's sometimes a little complicated. I try to play within my limits, as we say about a hockey player who concentrates on defence. Limit mistakes. Cause no suffering, or as little as possible, anyway, and to the smallest possible number of people. Starting there, life amounts to a simple question of arithmetic: either I make six people suffer, four of whom are totally innocent children, or else … Or else what, will you tell me? Is my life a long martyrdom, is it such a painful ordeal to live with a woman who's so beautiful she causes workplace accidents whenever she walks past a construction site? Aren't there worse kinds of suffering than living a life with her that resembles my sweetest dreams?

Okay, Cléo, time to go home. We'll go home and try to forget about all that. Maybe I should discuss it with Amélie, the expert at forgetting. If it's true that we can fill our heads with unicorns simply by repeating the word, why couldn't we reverse the process by repeating some silence, just enough silence to cover a person's first name?

MARITIMES

You know the kind of friend you want to see at times like that, the one to whom you tell everything? His name is Yves, and I've known him since college, when we worked together on a philosophy assignment. We got an excellent mark, which stunned us: Yves was the B type, like me, and our philosophy prof didn't really like management students, but believe me, we'd done a fantastic job of pretending to think the way he did. As well as the mark, we'd discovered that we got along really well and that we were more productive as a team than on our own — which always seems to me the exception, not the rule. And so we repeated the experiment as often as we could throughout our studies. We'd draw up the plan together, then Yves would work on the content and I on the form, and that was it. The confidence was mutual, the talents complementary, and besides that, we enjoyed ourselves. What more can a person ask? We lived through the ordeal of college together, then we met up again at university, where we dug the same trenches, shared the same mess tins, took the same accounting courses.

And there'd been that team project with Marie-France in an accounting course and then that wonderful April evening at her place ...

Yves had been the last to leave that night, and he was the one I called the next day, to tell him, or rather to give him to understand that I'd had a wonderful night. He'd congratulated me, which I'd always thought was a little inappropriate as a matter of fact; as if I had anything to do with it, as if I deserved the slightest credit ... But what else could he say? We congratulate lottery winners, after all ... And wasn't it just as inappropriate for me to phone my friend to announce my achievement? There's a good reason why the Lord made our mouths bigger than our eyes, as my grandmother used to say: when we see something we like, the most pressing thing to do is talk about it.

And so I wanted to talk about all that with him: Yves is my double, my parallel, my mirror image. Although he majored in partying at university, he finally married Diane, his first girlfriend, his first teenage love. He invited me to his wedding, I invited him to mine. They were a solid couple with children who arrived soon to consolidate it all. A marriage that keeps going, a marriage that's the envy of others. The attractive house on the South Shore, the growing children ... My double, I tell you. From the friend to whom you say everything, he quickly became the one to whom you say nothing, for the plain and simple reason that there was nothing to say: the mere fact that he existed was enough to reassure me.

After university, he didn't choose the public service like me, but Bell, which wasn't all that different, at the time anyway: a guaranteed job, a company as solid as a rock. But when he turned thirty he let himself be seduced by the sirens of adventure — professionally speaking — by moving to a smaller, more dynamic competitor, then to another even smaller, even more dynamic one, and so on until where does he end up but in the wonderful world of advertising? Working his fingers to the bone, three kids ... It was around that time that I lost sight of him a little, as was bound to happen. But a friend is still a friend, whether you see him or not.

I call him one Wednesday evening — my night off. A drink around five, what do you say? We'll avoid the bridges, replace rush hour with an hour or two of relaxation ... Phone home, call Yves again; we meet in a bar in Old Montreal, near the Court House, surrounded by lawyers who've spent all day talking and are still talking when evening comes, on the pretext of avoiding rush hour.

An imported beer, a big bowl of pretzels and we're off. Before the first drink is down, I've told him everything:

Marie-France and Josée, Josée and Marie-France ... We haven't yet ordered the second and I already know what he thinks. Our friendship is efficient.

"You aren't going to do that to me, are you," he says, alarmed. "Not you! You've always extolled the virtues of family, stability, security — you were kind of tiresome if you don't mind my saying so ..."

The trouble with old friends is that they aren't satisfied with giving you the opinion you ask for. Sometimes they overflow with opinions, they overproduce, and you don't know where to store them ... Tiresome, me? We'll see about that later. For now, I'm recording, it could come in handy.

"No, Marie-France is not just anybody, but that's not the point ... Nobody's just anybody, not Josée any more or any less than Marie-France ... It's just ... something you feel, something you know ... When Josée looks at me, I feel as if I'm breaking into a thousand pieces, as if I'm totally undone, and then the thousand pieces are welded together again right away, but differently, do you know what I mean? I'm totally destabilized. A different person altogether ..."

He nods, but he seems even more aghast. The more I try to explain, the more confused I am, and the more I feel that he's not listening to me. A moment later I toss the ball back to him, more to try extricating myself than to be polite.

"Hasn't it ever happened to you? Just between us ..."

"Oh, me ..."

And I see fog come to his eyes. A huge patch of fog. Enough to cover Newfoundland for one whole winter.

"Diane left me. That's why you haven't heard from me for a while. I hoped we could work things out. I hoped that things would go back to normal..."

"I'm sorry, I didn't know..."

It's my turn to be stunned. And to feel small, very small, when he tells me about the lawyers' letters and the custody arrangements, the friends who don't understand and who judge without knowing, the sleeping pills and other medication, and the nightmares that come back every night — nightmares in which his children fall one by one into a well, a bottomless well ... But I'll spare you the details: it's the kind of story you must know by heart because you've heard it a thousand times.

I go on feeling very small that evening on the drive home, and I repeat his advice as I'm crossing the bridge: "Don't do it, Marc. If you can avoid it, don't do it."

BUILDINGS

*T*he civil service. Undemanding work, lingering coffee breaks that stretch out, lunch hours that go on and on, hours spent arranging pencils according to size, automatic raises and iron-clad security — you know the song. But that's ancient history, going at least as far back as the 60s and 70s. By the early 80s there is already talk about imputability, productivity, efficiency. While the reality is still fairly peaceful, all things considered, the discourse is becoming more threatening and the pencil-pushing civil servant is having to make do with stubs. During the 90s we really get a taste of it, and I'm in a good position to know. It's cut after cut, and I'm not talking just about staplers and paper clips, but also about human beings. Layoffs, forced retirements, widespread anxiety. "You've given us twenty years of your life, thanks so much, we're really, really sorry, but ..." There they are, standing in front of you, and they're asking you why me, why not the other guy, and what will I do now, and the only answer you can give them is standards and budgets, clauses in collective agreements, rationalization ... No sooner are they out the door than you go right back to work, because there are more and more files and fewer and fewer people to process them, and also because it's better to work than to stop and think about what's happening to you.

Every morning at seven forty-five, I'm in the office, and it's not unusual for me to still be there at six-thirty. And then the meetings in Ottawa, the Saturdays at work to make up for lost time, gridlock on the bridges, to say nothing of the new vocabulary of the technocrats and computer analysts that never fails to open dizzying chasms beneath your feet: once you've decoded their lexicon, you still don't understand what it could possibly mean, and meanwhile you're behind again ...

All day long I'm running, and when I stop to catch my breath, I go to the window in my office and try to spot a patch of sky, a piece of cloud, a ray of sunlight, and I tell myself I've been had, somewhere or other. Why am I running, I who wanted to walk? I've always promised myself that I'd stay on top of my work and here I am as stressed-out as a bicycle messenger. I've always dreamed about having a decent job that would allow me to live and to eat and here I am with one that's eating me and keeping me from living. There's no way to put on the brakes or even to slow down. When you're on the highway you have to follow the traffic. And how far is it to the next exit?

If all the downtown buildings were made of mirrors, like the tower where Marie-France is cooped up, I could probably communicate with her by semaphore: she works downtown, a few blocks from my office. She runs too, faster and faster now that she's pushing forty, and even more since her parents' divorce. She runs because on the staircases of her building everybody runs, because no sooner do you try to slow down than someone's pushing you from behind. She runs to pay for the lawn and the garden shed, mortgage and taxes, private school and holidays, orthodontist and glasses, hockey and diving, babysitter and living room furniture, insurance and two cars … Sometimes, in the middle of the day, I feel like using semaphore to signal her, to talk to her about what we'd promised ourselves in university. Remember, Marie-France? We told each other not too fast, not too high, not too far. Family first, that's what we told each other …

But I can't signal to her by semaphore, any more than I can send her a carrier pigeon: where would it touch down on the twentieth storey of her glass building? And I long ago gave up on the phone: getting through the voice mail system only to end up with a secretary who tells me that Madame is in a meeting, thanks a lot, I skip my turn and go back to my files. Maybe that's where Marie-France and I lost one another, maybe that's what those glass buildings are designed for, maybe there are too many mirrors in our cities.

SESAME

Saturday morning, half past six. The sun's not up yet, cold rain is falling on the suburb, and I suspect that my windshield will soon be covered with a thick coating of ice that I'll have to scrape off; as soon as I've finished, I'll need to start again because it keeps falling, and my coat will be soaked with cold rain that will trickle down my back, but it doesn't matter, one must suffer to play hockey. In the meantime I try to unglue my eyelids with coffee, while keeping an eye on the odd little exercise that Mathieu performs when he makes his toast: as soon as the slice pops up, and before he spreads butter and jam, he brings it very close to his nose and sniffs it conscientiously, he actually inhales it, eyes closed.

"Smell good?"

"That depends ..."

"On what?"

"On lots of things. Near the crust it's often darker, so there's a burnt smell but it still smells good. When it isn't toasted at all it smells sugary, like fresh bread, but hotter. That smells *really* good. And when it's toasted just right, it smells fantastic, like caramel. Or butterscotch ice cream but hot, know what I mean? But of course it doesn't smell the same all the time. It depends on the toaster, for one thing, but mainly it depends on the bread. I don't like rye bread, it smells like kitty litter. But sesame seeds! Sometimes the seeds burst in the toaster and if you smell them right afterwards, it's awesome. Ordinary white bread without sesame seeds is good too, but it's better when it's just been sliced, and it's even better than that when it isn't sliced exactly right. That's because some parts of it stick out and they toast faster ..."

Then he tells me about hamburger buns and bagels, raisins and cinnamon, and I listen, fascinated, so fascinated by his masterly exposition that I forget to take notes.

"Don't you do that?" he asks me a moment later, amused at my surprise. "Don't you smell your toast in the morning?"

"No, not really. But I think I'll start. Meanwhile, buddy, we gotta get moving ..."

I gulp the rest of my coffee and go out to scrape off the ice that has built up on my car, and it's hard to be in a bad mood, even though circumstances demand it. Never mind the ice, never mind that the Kings are going to slaughter us once again: this morning, I have the very clear impression that my son has a genuine gift for happiness.

ॐ

Between the Christmas of the silk scarf and the Quebec Games, long years passed in the course of which I only saw Josée in homeopathic doses.

She's there sometimes, sitting in the bleachers at the rink, nose in a novel, while I pace behind the players' bench, eyes closed to keep from seeing the opposing team's tenth goal. When I open them again, once the disaster has passed, I barely notice Josée, barely look at her. But even that is enough to calm me down.

I run into her at the mall, strictly by chance, and we exchange a few platitudes, terribly embarrassed, as if we were guilty — but of what? Of running into each other by chance, of talking about the price of skates, of breathing the same polluted air?

Every time, I feel like staying there — anywhere, since it's with her — every time, I feel like talking about whatever comes into my head or even not talking at all, and every time I tell myself I mustn't. I look down, I look elsewhere, and I never know how to finish those conversations that don't even begin. I feel stupid, awkward, wrung out like a towel from which you want to squeeze the last drop.

And I talk to her on the phone, very often, too often, but always to tell her that I'll pick up/drive home Amélie and/or

Alex and/or Mathieu and/or Marie to take them/bring them back from the rink/the pool/the playground/school, and not to forget the skates/swimsuit/hairbrush/lunch/yellow dress/pyjamas, cross out whatever does not apply.

The tone is not that dry of course, but nearly. And when it isn't, then I'm using the saccharine tone I sometimes employ despite myself to keep from sounding dry. The tone is never right and every time, I'd like to continue the conversation — talk about this and that, as long as it's with her — every time I restrain myself, and every time I don't know what to say before I hang up. I always have the impression that the last silence went on too long, even when I've hung up too quickly.

Over the years I've never run into her in the extraordinary garden, though I'm a regular there. Though I've worn out all the paths in that park, I've always systematically avoided the one that leads to her house, often reflecting on the same thing: isn't doing my best not to go there to keep from thinking about her just another way of thinking about her, and is there a way to get out of that kind of reasoning?

All through those long years, only everyday matters, innocent matters, in infinitesimal quantities. And let me remind you that it's now been more than six years since we committed our worst infidelity, namely, touching hands, brushing fingertips in a restaurant in a mall, between two cardboard cups.

Not seeing one another to that degree when everything was urging us to do so was nearly indecent. But the waiting period was long enough for Marie-France to forget that there'd been an awkwardness, or at least to stop bringing it up. And if there'd been any awkwardness on Robert's part, that must have been blunted too, since no one made the slightest objection to our going to Baie-Comeau, Josée and me.

I didn't even have to be the one to decide. It happened by itself, quite naturally, like a cascade of dominoes: once the movement has started, there's nothing left to do but watch them fall.

At the beginning of the summer of 1993, we already knew that Marie had been chosen for the Quebec Games, which were taking place in Baie-Comeau. If you're familiar with such events, you know that the children travel by bus with their delegation and sleep in local schools. It's all beautifully organized, so I didn't need to go there with my daughter. But Marie had just squeaked in, and most likely this would be her last important competition. I'd have felt bad if I didn't attend. Since I had a few days of unclaimed vacation and a wonderful pretext for using them, why not go too? I don't mind distance driving now and then, as long as the road is very long, so long that I can forget that I have to arrive somewhere. As a way to take your mind off something, it's nearly as good as walking.

Marie-France didn't have any unclaimed vacation days. And as she still couldn't bear to watch her children in a competition — in fact she could bear it less and less as her own work became competitive — the question didn't even arise. And finally, since Mathieu and Alex would be at camp, Marie-France thought of my trip as a kind of holiday: the big house would be empty for five days, she'd have four evenings of total freedom to eat with women friends or watch *Gone with the Wind* once again while nibbling nachos, or spend hours in the tub and reread *Jane Eyre* …When you have kids, you relish pleasures like that. Four long evenings of freedom? That's called Paradise.

And so it was decided: I would go to Baie-Comeau by myself, like a big boy, I'd take Marie's photo with her gold medal, and then I'd make my unhurried way home. And maybe — why not? — maybe I'd spend a day in Quebec City…

But that was without taking account of Marie, who had other plans. While Marie-France and I were talking about the trip, our daughter bounced into the kitchen, from who knows where. (Marie never walks: she jumps, she bounces, she runs. Except of course when we want to take her somewhere and she doesn't want to go. When that happens, she drags her feet — if she isn't actually ramming them into the ground.)

"That's not fair: Alex and Mathieu have their camp, I've got my competition, and Amélie hasn't got anything."

No need to say a word to divine Marie-France's opinion. A glance is enough.

"Sure, she could come along. We'd have to talk to her parents…"

Before I've finished my sentence, Marie is climbing the stairs four at a time, and before I catch my breath she's back down, even faster: how on earth can she come down the stairs without touching a single step?

"Josée's on the phone. She wants to talk to you."

Marie-France takes the call and I hear only bits of their conversation.

"That's just what we were saying … Yes, we thought so too … Hard to do otherwise … Same here … Of course … Look, he's right here, you can talk to him …"

She hands me the receiver and I listen to Josée repeat to me, probably word for word, that she's talked it over with Robert and they both think it's normal for Amélie to want to go to Baie-Comeau and cheer for her best friend. Robert can't get away but she just promised her daughter that she'll take her. Besides, it will be good for her, this little trip before school starts … But since I'm going too … We won't take two cars, that would be silly…

"It would be silly," agrees Marie-France at my side.

"It would be silly," says Robert too when he comes on the line. "The two of you, I mean the three of you ought to go. I've even got the name of a nice little inn near Baie-Comeau. But you'd have to reserve right away, the town will be crawling with parents … Poor you, can't you see it, a town full of parents with noisemakers? Good luck! Here's Josée again while I look up the number ..."

A trip to Baie-Comeau. On a silver platter. With the blessing of Robert and Marie-France ... It's a little hard to believe, I confess. While waiting for Robert to come back I have to talk with Josée and I can't think of anything to say except to repeat the same refrain, over and over: it would be ridiculous not to drive up together, in fact it makes sense, we'll share expenses, it would be silly to take two cars, really silly... Eventually Josée tells me that Robert can't seem to find the number of his inn, but that she'll book the rooms as soon as he does. We'll leave Friday morning, early, let's say eight o'clock?

"Let's say eight o'clock, yes."

I said eight o'clock but I could just as well have said *deck chair* or *icing sugar* if she'd asked me to. There are certain circumstances when you say something because you have to say something, because that's what people do, because you can't just stand there holding the phone and saying nothing; there are circumstances in which you talk but the words have absolutely no meaning.

"Friday morning, eight o'clock ..."

"Is it going to work?" asks Marie as soon as I've hung up.

"Sure it's going to work."

Marie can't stand still, she hops up and down, jumps on the sofa, stays there two seconds, squirming so much that all the cushions move, then she bounces to the kitchen where she opens and shuts all the cupboard doors without finding anything that satisfies her, goes back to the living room where she wriggles on a chair long enough to turn on the TV, zap all fifty stations — twenty seconds are all she needs — and switch it off, then gets up and races to her room to phone Amélie.

That was Marie, in excited mode. Marie-in-a-flurry, Marie-the-whirlpool, Marie-Superball. Thank you, Marie, thank you for giving me this distraction. Thank you for convincing us, if we needed convincing, that we really couldn't do otherwise.

⁓

Seven o'clock Thursday morning. No question about it, my Mathieu gets me up early. Not for hockey this time, for summer camp. It was agreed that I'd pick up Alex and drive both boys to their bus. And while we're waiting we both conscientiously sniff our toast.

I still do that. And when I forget, I spend a bad day every time. Systematically.

"What do you think of this one?"

Since I consider myself a novice in this matter, I wait impatiently for the expert's verdict. Mathieu shuts his eyes and inhales slowly, religiously.

"Super awesome. It's the sesame seeds. But maybe you could have left it in a little longer..."

I sniff my slice of bread again, resigned. I'll never be an expert, I don't think: time dulls the sense of smell ...

"Who showed you how to do that, by the way?"

"That what?"

And that's Mathieu: two seconds are all he needs to sail off to the clouds, explore them inside out, and then come back — when he does come back. He's definitely much slower than his sister, is Mathieu, but it's a good kind of slowness and I envy it. No doubt he'll never play pro hockey, but as a dreamer, let me tell you ...

"Who showed you how to inhale your toast in the morning?"

"Josée. She's got this amazing toaster. You ought to try it some time."

THE ROAD WAS LONG

THE CURSE OF
THE COMBINE HARVESTER

*W*henever I'm a humble passenger in an automobile, my old hitchhiking reflexes come back: I talk, I ask questions, I converse, in short I make the maximum noise to entertain the driver, or at least to keep him awake. Such is the price to pay in exchange for transportation without opening one's purse. And yet it wasn't to avoid boredom that Josée had me get into her car, still less was it out of charity, but even so I start talking as soon as the car door is shut, and I'm still talking as we approach Drummondville. The words emerge from my mouth almost despite myself, and show the extent of my discomfort. Talk about whatever comes to mind while doing my best to include Amélie in the conversation. Is it not for her, is it not thanks to her, that we're here?

With Josée, fortunately, there's nothing easier than making those desultory remarks that come to us so easily in a car, as long as we let logic take a break. We allow ourselves to be carried along by the words and it's only later, much later, that we realize our remarks only seemed to be desultory, that they actually corresponded to another logic.

The sky is the kind of blue that's only seen in August, light and translucent, yet our casual chatter always took us to the dark side of things. Perhaps at first we'd spotted a crow or a red-winged blackbird or a grackle, one of those black birds that loot other birds' nests and that are sometimes victims in turn of air raids by much smaller birds ... I know that we talked about birds for a long time and probably brought up Hitchcock before we branched off in the direction of vultures, wars and battlefields. After that we moved on to bats, then vampires, and that was how, along the way, we arrived at ghosts and poltergeists.

It would be an understatement to say that Amélie was interested in the subject: she was absolutely fascinated, overexcited even. How could she not be, at the age of twelve? She even told us that the sister of one of her friends had powers of telekinesis and telepathy: every night while she was asleep objects on her dresser would move around, very noisily if she was on the outs with her mother. She also felt as if she could read her mother's mind like a book, and could even *act on* what she read ...

Josée and I listened to her story, which Amélie seemed absolutely convinced was true, then we served up the arguments that all good parents who entertain a healthy degree of scepticism would use in such circumstances: it doesn't take much to make an object move on a dresser, vibrations caused by a truck driving past, for instance; reading a mother's mind is definitely an exploit, but the coefficient of difficulty diminishes significantly if the mother is angry; everyone would like to believe in such phenomena, everyone would like to believe in the power of his or her mind, everyone would like to believe, period, but there isn't the tiniest hint of proof that such phenomena have ever existed ...

And why shouldn't the mind have such powers, retorted Amélie, isn't it true that we only use a very small part of our brain, and anyway, how can you prove that something doesn't exist?

If we were able to convince Amélie of anything that day, it was that we were not merely narrow-minded, but we were also terrible spoilsports, and most likely she'd have sulked for the rest of the trip if Josée, rather than pursuing her lecture on Realism 101, hadn't started to tell us a strange story about an experience she'd had at the age of thirteen, when she'd spent a week with one of her cousins who lived in the country. She had seen there things so strange, phenomena so inexplicable, that she really had believed, that summer, in the existence of supernatural powers.

Josée was in a story-telling mood, you could tell from the way that she settled into her seat, wriggling and coughing to clear her throat, the way we do when we're getting ready to talk at length. At the same time, she was preparing her audience: this story is going to be long, I'll take the time to create the atmosphere, without neglecting any detail ... It's unnecessary to add that we were very willing to listen to her: on the road from Montreal to Quebec City, any distraction is good. Go for it, Josée.

Josée was thirteen, then, and she was invited to spend a week at her cousin Rachel's, a cousin she didn't know very well and had never really trusted. Rachel was very thin, with shifty eyes. She always seemed to be afraid of something. When the girls went for walks in the forest or the fields, Rachel would often turn around sharply, as if she were afraid she was being followed. Even more worrying, she was behaving that way at home now: how could anyone have come upon her by surprise from behind when her back was always right against the wall, whether in the kitchen or the living room? And her bed was as far from the window as possible, but that didn't stop her from getting up often, with a start, in the middle of the night, to scan the darkness ...

How to detect the signs of a lie in a person who's wearing dark glasses and who has to keep her eyes on the road? Was her story true, in full or in part, or was Josée making it up as she went along, which was what I suspected? No matter:

when a story is good you don't ask yourself if it's true. What you do is keep quiet and listen.

… Nothing is more contagious than fear. If cousin Rachel was worried enough to be upsetting, Rachel's father was downright scary. Since the death of his wife, he had lived alone with his daughter on that isolated farm in the middle of nowhere. He worked all day, ate like an ogre, then he went to sleep and that was that. His only leisure activity was to sit in his rocking chair in the evening and smoke an interminable pipe. This uncle never said a word to anyone, he communicated by mumbling. How could Rachel figure out what her father wanted? It was very mysterious. The uncle muttered, and Rachel would get him some milk. He'd add a vague grunt, she'd pass him the salt. The uncle too was always being startled and he'd race to the window to peer at the horizon, even though nothing ever appeared there. So what were Rachel and her father afraid of? As far as the eye could see there was nothing but rolling fields. Could it be that, at night, they could sometimes spot a wolf or a coyote in the moonlight, or admire a bat in flight …

I look at Josée, whose eyes are glued to the road directly ahead of her. I can tell that she's laying it on a little thick with her wolves and her bats, but there's still no way to know if she's embellishing a story that may have some basis in fact, or if she's leading us up the garden path. Ah perfidious Josée, who's taking advantage of the hazards of the road to stoke the suspense: every time she passes a convoy of semi-trailers, she breaks off her story for safety's sake. Which means that she can keep us waiting as she wishes, a pleasure that she doesn't deny herself.

… Everything in that house was so sad: not the slightest bit of colour or the smallest decoration, no knick-knacks, not even a calendar or a photo pinned to the wall, nothing but that which was stupidly practical, like the pots and pans hanging from nails in the kitchen and the rifle above the fireplace …

I glance at Amélie while we're passing another convoy of semis: she's so captivated that her whole body is straining towards the front, as far as her seat belt will allow. I look at Josée, in search of even a hint, a sign of complicity, but nothing. These convoys of semi-trailers can be awfully long …

… One night, consumed with worry and unable to sleep, Josée gets up for a glass of water. Though she makes herself very small, very light, all the floors in this old house creak and crack. It must have been those sounds that warned her uncle of her presence, there's no other possible explanation: when she gets to the living room, she sees that his chair is still moving, as if a ghost were rocking in it. Not only is it moving, it's actually moving faster and faster, contrary to all logic. Suddenly, Josée hears a horrible scream upstairs. She races up four stairs at a time. When she gets to the bedroom the window is wide open and her cousin's bed is empty. Rachel has disappeared …

There's one more truck to pass, and then another that passes us, making such a racket that conversation is impossible. When it finally disappears, by some miracle the road is absolutely clear. No sign of a truck or even a motorcycle to interrupt Josée's story. Yet she falls silent. Everyone will agree that silence is an important weapon in the storyteller's arsenal, but even so, you mustn't go too far.

"Then what happened?" asks Amélie finally, out of patience.

"Do you really want to know the rest?" replies Josée.

"Of course I do! What happened to Rachel?"

"I'm warning you: if you really want to know, I'll have to tell you the truth, nothing but the truth. And the truth may be..."

"Stop!" Amélie interrupts her. "You're going to tell me you made it all up from the beginning, or that Rachel had got up to go to the bathroom and the screams came from an owl ... I know your stories!"

It is as if Amélie's seat belt had been turned into an elastic that had snapped her back to her seat, where she is getting ready to sulk for the rest of the trip, not without reason for that matter: who ever heard of leaving a story like that in mid-stream?

"We could think of another ending," I say. "Josée goes to the window and the only thing she sees is a rusted-out old tractor..."

"... and the tractor starts to move," Amélie goes on, and her face reappears between the seats.

"I'd prefer a combine harvester if I have the choice," Josée steps in. "Imagine dozens of long rusty teeth lit by moonlight … And Rachel a prisoner of the machine …"

"A combine harvester possessed by an evil spirit. Didn't Stephen King write something like that?"

"There used to be a graveyard on the property …" Amélie takes over without answering my question.

"A mass grave, a battlefield …"

"And the uncle's a ghost and he can make the combine harvester obey him …"

"I've got the title: *The Curse of the Combine Harvester*. Don't you think that sounds good?"

The Curse of the Combine Harvester had us on tenterhooks nearly all the way to Quebec City. When we came to the rest stop where we got out and stretched our legs, we decided to leave the dread machine there before it overindulged on little girls. I of course took advantage of Amélie's going to buy a chocolate bar from a vending machine to approach Josée with the question I've been dying to ask.

"Are you making up your story as you go?"

"Of course. I was grateful when you came to my rescue. I've always liked open-ended stories. As long as the end isn't written, you can always go on inventing."

I stopped breathing: there was Josée, who had taken off her dark glasses and was looking me squarely in the eyes, perfectly well aware of what she was saying. There was Josée, and me, in the parking lot at this rest stop, and every word sounded like a promise.

And Amélie, who was gobbling a Coffee Crisp without the slightest remorse, after inventing a combine harvester that dug up corpses in graveyards.

"Still, it's strange that we're telling horror stories when the sky is so blue," said Josée when we were back in the car.

Maybe she'd once been a hitchhiker too: now that I was driving, she felt obliged to make conversation.

We went on to talk about the colour of the sky and its influence on our moods, about the patterns made by clouds and about certain winds that drive people crazy, and our meteorological preoccupations soon made us branch off to our favourite songs: we called up Brassens' *little bit of umbrella we can trade in for a bit of paradise and the rain that falls and carefully weighs its drops on the wedding, the rain that falls on Nantes that fills my heart with woe, and remember, Barbara, it was raining over Brest that day* ...

The bluer the sky became — blue as it can only be in August — the more we sang about the rain, and the further back we searched our memories. That poem by Verlaine, how did it go?

> It rains in my heart
> As it rains on the town
> What languor seeps in
> Where my heart is undone

When we arrived at the Tadoussac ferry we had exhausted our repertoire of rain songs, including Boy Scout numbers and the inevitable "Singin' in the Rain," which we'd sung in chorus at the top of our lungs.

Amélie, absolutely disgusted, had long since plugged herself into her Walkman.

I sneaked a glance at her now and then: sunk back in her seat as deeply as possible, she was listening to a heavy metal tape while leafing through an Archie comic and cuddling a teddy bear. There's nothing more perplexing than a twelve-year-old girl.

Once we were past the Saguenay, conversation flagged. Now there were just small pockets of words with longer and longer spaces between them. We gave up the struggle, conceded victory to the silence and the road, which sometimes presented us with glorious views of the St. Lawrence. Tadoussac, Les Escoumins, Sault-au-Mouton, Saint-Paul-du-Nord, Betsiamites, Papinachois ... The landscapes that stretched out, the bewildering names, the vast sky that took up more and more space as the trees got smaller ... I felt as if I were discovering a foreign country.

Josée is driving again and I let myself drift into daydreams.

Her name, let's say, was Sylvie. Her name was Sylvie and she was my girlfriend, not to say my first love. We were sixteen and we would kiss for hours on the living-room sofa. Whole Saturday nights of kissing and nothing else, and never tiring.

To tell the truth I didn't really want to "go any further." Maybe, quite simply, because I was scared.

Her name, let's say, was Sylvie, and we spent every Saturday night kissing. I would caress her hands, her neck, her back and sometimes her breasts — through her sweater. One evening when her parents were out, she'd slowly unbuttoned her blouse and let me caress her naked breasts, breasts that were very small, but that occupied a huge space in my memory, so small and so beautiful, so soft, so warm ... I still ask myself how I was able to survive that experience: never had my heart beat so hard, never had my ribs been subjected to so much pressure, never had I felt such inner ferment ...

Why am I thinking about that now? Is it those memories that are making my heart beat faster, or is it being here, in this automobile, next to Josée?

"Can I ask you something, mama?" inquires Amélie, speaking much too loud as if to drown out the music from her Walkman, though only she can hear it.

"Of course," replies Josée, who also seems to be coming back from far away.

"It's about the rocking chair ..."

Thank you, Amélie. Thank you for giving me something else to think about, and thank you for putting the rocking chair back on the table, so to speak. It really was the best part of her story, that rocking chair swaying back and forth all by itself, faster and faster. How will Josée extricate herself from that one? Either she admits that her story was pure fiction or she's condemned to make up a new law of physics on the spot...

"You really want to know the truth?" asks Josée.

"No, no, I don't. It's just that I'm trying to see the word *rocking* in my head and I know that sometimes there's a little line between two words that joins them together and I can't remember what you call it."

"That little line is called a hyphen."

"Hyphen, hyphen, hyphen — that's right, that's the word that disappeared ... Hyphen..."

Thank you, Amélie, thank you for that hyphen that joins together two words.

ON THE WHARF

*H*ere's your key," says the motel's young receptionist, a girl with red curls who looks not much older than Amélie. "And this one is for Mademoiselle ..."

We have to explain that's not quite right, that Madame and Mademoiselle will be sleeping in the same room, while Monsieur ...

"That doesn't make any difference," replies the young woman, shrugging conspicuously to let us know that our private life is none of her business. The rooms communicate. That's to allow for ...

The rooms communicate? That doesn't make any difference, obviously. We haven't come to Baie-Comeau to do summer theatre, with to-ings and fro-ings and concertos of slamming doors, but still, there is something improper about that door between the two rooms. *That's to allow for* ... the young woman had said. Allow for what exactly? And by whom?

Josée and Amélie have gone to their room and I am exploring mine. The curtains are heavy, the walls are covered with fake walnut panelling, and the massive furniture is also made of fake walnut. Why are motel rooms always so dark? So that stains won't show so badly, I suppose. Saves on upkeep. As if all that weren't stodgy enough, the air is saturated with the clinging smell of stale tobacco and detergent. But the Quebec Games are on, there were no vacancies at the inn Robert suggested, and all the hotels in town are chock-full of parents, so we take what there is and make do. Anyway, there are better things to do than complain: open the window for instance, knock on the shared door to ask the girls how things are on their side and visit each other's room, which are of course exactly the same, isn't that amazing, but it shifts the air around, especially when Amélie jumps on each of the beds to test them. Thank you Amélie, for mixing the atmospheres in our two rooms.

Each of us then returns to his quarters for a shower: an eight-hour drive makes for plenty of dust to wash off the body, plenty of fatigue to sluice away.

When I'm taking my clothes off I can hear everything on the other side: first the creaking of the beds, which Amélie is still having fun trying out, then the TV, the drawers opening and closing, and finally the bathroom taps ... Then I climb into the shower and I don't know if the water that's playing a percussion ensemble on the plastic wall is coming from me or from them. A little more and I could hear the soap caressing Josée's skin, the bubbles gliding over her ...

It's so awkward that I cut short my ablutions and arrive early at the reception desk where we've arranged to meet. While I wait for the girls I flip through one of those tourist guides you always find in hotels, in case I might discover some pleasant way to spend the few hours before the opening ceremony, but all I see are photos of monster lobsters and gargantuan steaks, lush golf courses, and buxom beauties lounging by a pool. I could be in Miami Beach, Boston or Toronto and it would be just the same: wide-angle photos of the same hotel rooms and occasionally a local feature, a finback whale or a dolphin, starring this week at the municipal aquarium ...

"What are you looking for?" asks Josée, radiant in her summer dress. "There's never anything in those guides ..."

I'm not sure what to say in reply. Because ...

Because I'm bowled over. I wasn't expecting to see her when I looked up. And especially not in a summer dress. It's the very first time I've seen her in a dress, at least I think so, and it gives her a playful look, a holiday look. I would like to tell her that she's beautiful, that she smells good, I'd like to take her by the hand and turn her around to make her dress swirl, but I don't say a word and maybe it's not really necessary anyway: she just has to look at me to see how I'm looking at her, how my eyes linger on her, how they have trouble looking away. Trying to force myself to think about something else, I stammer something.

"I was looking for a map of the town ... Usually, the first thing I visit in a place I don't know is the graveyard..."

"The graveyard?" says Amélie, who's at Josée's side and has just made a face.

I spoke a little too loudly, it seems, because the young receptionist has looked up from her magazine to ask the same question.

"The graveyard?"

I understand their reaction: at their age it's perfectly normal. But as Josée is also looking at me strangely, I feel obliged to explain that I'm neither a vampire nor a necrophile, that graveyards are often very pleasant places for a walk, and you can also enjoy an accelerated history lesson: you see Irish names take over from Scots, ordinary Englishmen marrying francophone Catholics, you see children dying very young from the Spanish flu...

"That's all very interesting," says Josée, "but we're in Baie-Comeau."

"So?"

"This town is so young it may not even have a graveyard ..."

"Come on, we aren't *that* young!" says the receptionist, visibly shocked. "Our graveyard may be young, but it's just as interesting as any other ..."

"I'm sure it is," says Josée kindly, anxious to avoid a diplomatic incident, "but it seems to me it would be more interesting to go for a walk on the wharf, wouldn't it?"

"Absolutely!" says the young woman, friendly again. "You won't be sorry … Take Lasalle Boulevard just across the way, then you …"

Okay, the wharf.

Okay, the wharf, and what a good idea: it's much longer than I'd have imagined, with freighters and tugs, cranes and containers, but also with lone anglers, like you always see on wharves along the St. Lawrence. I've always admired the silence of fishermen and their very special way of letting time slip by.

We walk unhurriedly to the end of the wharf and from there we try to catch sight of the other shore, without success. There is nothing but the river, nothing but the sea. We're on a wharf, an immense concrete wharf, yet if we look at the horizon we can feel ourselves going away, we embark on a huge ship heading for the open sea, we're floating along and we can no longer see the shore, we've left real life behind … You know how a person feels after an eight-hour drive: a little like a zombie, brains in a stew, thoughts bobbing up and down … I am stunned from the road and intoxicated by the sea air; I can't find any other explanation for what happened next. I didn't even think about it. If I had thought, I never would have dared. It's because I didn't think that I did what I did, quite unconsciously.

To the others on the Baie-Comeau wharf that day, we are just a man and a woman who aren't from there, an ordinary tourist couple who've come here to gaze at the sea. A couple looking into the distance, very far away, whose daughter is getting impatient: I'm hungry, when are we going to have supper?

I didn't think about it for even a quarter of a second, I swear, or I'd never have had the nerve to do what I did. I was still dazed from the journey, there's no other explanation. When Amélie starts walking to the car, I go up to Josée and put my hands on her shoulders, from the back. I just want to keep her there for a moment, to steal a little of her time. It doesn't feel as if I'm betraying or being unfaithful to anyone, I don't know what I'm doing, I don't know who she is or who I am, and at the same time I feel as if I'm doing what I have to do.

She was there, getting ready to join her daughter after she'd looked at the river, and I put my hands on her shoulders, very gently, very naturally; and as she didn't move, and as she'd done nothing to break away from me, I placed my lips on her shoulder — without even touching her skin, just her dress, and it was quite an achievement not to touch her skin, given the width of the shoulder strap — I just placed my lips on her dress, that's all, without the slightest premeditation, I swear, without the slightest intention, it was an automatic move, I touched my lips to her shoulder, to the fabric of her dress, and I realized that it was her, that it was Josée, and that it was me, and that I had no right to do it.

I stepped back right away, as if I'd had an electric shock.

"Sorry, I don't know what came over me; the driving maybe, I feel like a zombie…"

She stammered something too, but I confess, I didn't understand a word.

KNOCK THREE TIMES

While I sometimes follow the Olympics or the Pan-American games on TV, I never watch opening ceremonies. Speeches and flags, mayors and MPs climbing onto the podium and congratulating each other, the government ministers who come along to oust them, and all those potbellied individuals singing the praises of sports and youth while the young people file past them like soldiers — the whole thing is quite simply indecent. Politics sucks the blood out of everything, it's absolutely shameless. And then there are the young girls who are required to run while carrying long banners, and the booming music that echoes endlessly off the stadium walls — an absolute horror. The horrors are all there in Baie-Comeau, but rougher, more amateur, which is actually not bad. And besides, if you're a parent you don't see any of the opening ceremony, you don't hear the brass bands, you don't see anything except your child, and you're deaf to everything else: there she is, look, there's Marie, in the third row, there she is! It's her! It's my daughter! It's Marie!

I wave my arms to get her attention, a moment later Josée and Amélie do the same, but Marie is much too far away. How could she make us out from all the hysterical parents who also only have eyes for their child? Her delegation creeps along at a snail's pace but we go on waving our arms until she finally spots us when she draws level with us. My eyes meet hers and she waves her arms faster and faster, so fast that she's liable to take flight when she finally spots Amélie; she stamps her feet, she jumps up and down, and Amélie also stamps and jumps, as if they were both taking a run-up so they could meet in the pennants hanging from the ceiling of the arena.

This one moment makes the whole trip worthwhile. Our daughters lock eyes with one another and all at once I feel myself overflowing with leniency: bring on the speeches, stretch out your ceremony, I'm sure that in the end I'll think it was all beautiful — even the music that's bouncing off the cement walls.

Marie has gone past us now and all we can see is her back. I turn to Josée to tell her I don't know what, but I'm mute. Every time, it will be the same, every time, she'll take my breath away, every time, I'll be just as astonished at finding her there, and I'll ask myself every time if I'm dreaming, if I really am here in Baie-Comeau, with her.

You know that sense of unreality you often experience on the first day of a trip, as if the body has travelled faster than your ideas, as if your memory hasn't had time to adjust? You're there but you feel as if you're elsewhere, as in a dream. From that point to the idea that anything can happen, that anything is allowed ... That must be what happened a while ago, on the wharf. It's because of travel, because of the road. And there's the fact that everyone sees us as Amélie's parents, and everything is confused ...

I'm still not altogether back to normal when the ceremony ends and Marie is climbing up the bleachers, bouncing rather, from row to row, like a mountain goat, to come and join us. We've no sooner embraced than she turns to Amélie, all fired up.

"There's room in the school and there's an extra sleeping bag and I asked Élisabeth, she says it's okay, you can come and sleep with us. There's Élisabeth, you know her, and there's Catherine and Maude and Audrey, we'll make room for you ..."

And then she turns to me: say yes, papa, say yes, say yes, say yes, at the same time Amélie turns to her mother: say yes, mama, say yes, say yes, say yes ...

"Do you really want to?" Josée asks her daughter, as if the question needs to be posed.

Amélie doesn't even reply, but we can read the answer in her eyes: I've got a choice between staying in a motel with my mother or in a school gym with my friends? Come on, mama …

Josée gives me a questioning look, I reply with a shrug: what do you want me to say? You decide.

"Okay. Shall we go to the motel and get your clothes?"

There's an explosion of joy in our daughters' hearts while at the same time anxiety sweeps over me. I'll have to drink some water, I've never felt so hot, my throat has never been so dry.

~

We didn't even have to drive them back to the school where they're being put up. Élisabeth did that, since she's in charge of all the formalities. Clothes and toothbrush, pyjamas and Walkman are collected. The backpack is in the trunk of Élisabeth's taxi pronto, and the two friends on the back seat. They hardly break off their chatter to wave goodbye when the taxi drives out of the parking lot.

Before the tail lights have even disappeared on the horizon, for our daughters we've stopped existing. There are just Josée and me in the parking lot, lit by the neon lights of the motel. Josée and me, alone, and we'll exist a little too much.

A while ago, on the wharf, I felt drained after the long trip. Now I feel full, too full: my head is too full of words, so that I no longer know which one to use, my body is too full of matter, and I don't even know how to move.

"What time is it?" asks Josée.

I feel like thanking her: thank you for saying something.

"Ten o'clock …"

"It's a little early to go to sleep. We could have a drink — or just walk for a while."

"Sure, let's walk. We spent all day in the car and all evening in an arena, I don't really feel like being inside some noisy place."

"Okay then, let's walk. But I have to call Robert first. I promised I'd call around ten."

"Good idea. I'll call home too and we'll meet back here in five minutes?"

જી

If it took eight hours to get from Longueuil to Baie-Comeau, I only need a few seconds to go back to Longueuil. Time enough to punch in a number, hear the phone ring …

"Hello," says Marie-France and I'm surprised to hear her voice. I feel as if I'm speaking to a stranger on the other side of the world.

I tell her about the trip, she tells me about her day, and I sense that she's closer and closer, more and more familiar. I talk about Marie, about how pretty she looked among the hundreds of children in the procession, she talks about the big house, how empty it is since we left, about the big house that's become an echo chamber for the crickets' concert …

She says, listen; she stops talking, and I can hear the crickets, and there I am, instantly, back in that house in the suburbs where the crickets sing so loudly in August that we sometimes turn off the television in the evening, to listen to them. It sounds as if there are thousands of them along the foundations, and we keep wondering if it's true that Japanese children raise crickets as pets in tiny cages. We've always liked crickets, Marie-France and I. From August till October, when they go numb for the winter, there is no reason why anyone needs sleeping pills.

I listen to the crickets, then I listen again to Marie-France's voice while she wishes me good night, and as a result I get all my memory back and so I can no longer pretend that I'm someone else.

I hang up and listen to the silence for a long time: there are no crickets in Baie-Comeau yet, or maybe they haven't started to sing. I stay in that silence and now I'm neither in Baie-Comeau nor in Longueuil: I am nowhere, the way that a motel room can make you feel that you're nowhere. I stay in that silence, not daring to get up, until I hear the sound of water in the bathroom pipes. I imagine that Josée has phoned Robert and that she's now getting ready to go out.

I join her outside, where she's looking at the stars. I gaze at them with her. Her head in the sky but both feet on the ground: she can't pretend to be someone else now either. We can no longer cheat, no longer pretend: we live on the same very small planet, in the same space-time continuum, and it's very small too.

We walk in the deserted town for a long time that evening, without ever touching, even accidentally. We zigzag along the streets of Baie-Comeau, trying not to stray too far from Lasalle Boulevard, and it's when we are retracing our steps, as I imagine it, that I'm able to tell her the source of my fondness — my insatiable appetite, rather — for walking.

I was thirteen, maybe fourteen years old, I was at Uncle Léo's chalet with my parents, and I was bored the way only a thirteen- or fourteen-year-old can be bored — which is to say, extremely. It felt to me as if time was going to stop for good, that I was going to be stuck in it as if it were asphalt liquefied by the heat. Instead of staying there doing nothing, I'd decided to walk to the village. Just like that, for no reason. On a whim. I got up, I put one foot in front of the other, and I left. I walked for two miles, as we used to say back then, which is somewhere around six or seven kilometres, round trip. There was nothing spectacular along the road — trees, swamps, fences and barns, some dented hubcaps in the ditch — but even so I enjoyed it. Why? The mere fact of being in motion, I imagine, of being obliged to look at whatever there was to look at, to think differently, with no ties, no moorings. "Too bad," my father told me when I got back to the chalet around noon. "If I'd known you were going to the village, I'd have asked you to buy me cigarettes..."

It didn't matter to me and, to his amazement, I set out again. The same walk, with the same barns, the same fences, the same dented hubcaps in the same ditches. I brought back my father's cigarettes, I had supper with the family, and that evening I returned to the village for the third time. Still the same fences and the same barns, but each time I noticed a different detail, and the colours were never the same, or the taste of the air — to say nothing of my daydreams ...

My brothers and cousins said I was crazy when I finally came back at nightfall. But is it any crazier to walk than to spend the day carving pieces of wood, or reading detective stories, or doing nothing? I didn't feel as if I was going crazy, no. I felt calm and fulfilled, I had the impression that I'd found myself the way someone else may have the impression that he's found himself with his very first experience of painting or theatre or driving a truck ... The impression that it was what I'd always wanted, that I'd been waiting for that day forever ... I was thirteen or fourteen years old and I knew that whatever happened to me, I could always simply leave instead of feeling stuck. With time, it has become one of the two or three certainties I most care about. Walk. Leave my problems behind and walk. Find them again on my return, of course, but look at them with a new eye. I just have to put one foot in front of the other ...

"What were you dreaming about?"

"Love, I imagine ..."

"Tell me ..."

"At that age, I imagined meeting someone just like that, by chance, someone who would be walking towards me ... I imagined a face, not a body, eyes, not lips ... It was very pure, very intangible ... Maybe that day was even the first time I let myself dream about a great love. Maybe I had to walk for hours to start up the hormone dispenser and maybe that's why I remember it so clearly ..."

There is a long silence, which I don't dare to disturb. Josée is walking more and more slowly, and I adapt my pace to hers. I imagine her lost in thought, revisiting her own adolescent dreams, perhaps reliving her first loves, who knows? Do other people's stories always take us back to our own? She too must have had her share of bungalow basement loves, of kisses stolen with the complicity of the rain, under a car shelter, after the prom ...

"I never had a teenage love," she says finally, after a very long moment. "And I've always regretted it."

"You never fell in love at fifteen?"

"Not at fifteen, and not at sixteen or seventeen or eighteen ... The first man in my life was thirty-seven. I was twenty-one. He was married. A secret affair that lasted for a few years ... The second one was forty. Also married. And the third was Robert."

"And before that nothing?"

"Absolutely nothing. I wasn't interested in the boys my age and I imagine the feeling was mutual. We lived on different planets, I think. I suppose that luck, bad luck, played its part too, but never mind. I never had a sixteen-year-old love, at least not until I met you."

I feel her remark penetrate to the nucleus of every cell in my body, where it still echoes now, seven years later.

"That time our fingertips touched, at Place Longueuil, that was what I thought of right away: I was never in love when I was sixteen and now it's happening to me. Life is playing tricks on me: it's turning back the clock, it's going backwards. Once upon a time there was a girl of sixteen who listened to the same records in her room a hundred times and knew every song by Jacques Brel and Reggiani and Boris Vian by heart and who dreamed and dreamed ... Years later, life sends her someone who knows the same songs, someone who knows that *the stairs on the Butte are hard on the poor*, who has visited *that grey square where a blind man played the barrel organ* ... Here I am an adult, and life sends me my teenage love ... There's been a mistake somewhere. Whose fault is it? I don't know ... It's like the stories you read in the papers now and then about letters delivered twenty years late ... I was never in love at sixteen and I've always regretted it. I thought it would be you but ..."

"But?"

"But it's impossible, you know that as well as I do. Our daughters are twelve years old. Soon it'll be their turn to walk down the streets in pairs, like all the girls and boys their age ... And then it will be Alex and Mathieu's turn ..."

And what if we were to try to stop time? I touch her hand lightly and she doesn't say anything. I take her hand, her hand that feels so cool, while I feel as if I'm boiling.

"And what if we were sixteen?" I say. "Sixteen years old, for a few days …"

"Sixteen …" she murmurs.

I stop, I pull her to me, but she resists.

"Sixteen years old," she says. "I don't want us to go any further…"

"It's amazing what you can allow yourself to do when you're sixteen …"

"In that case, let's say thirteen."

All right, thirteen.

We go back to the motel holding hands and humming songs by Françoise Hardy. When I leave her at her door I take a chance and kiss her. Not on the lips, no. I simply put my hands on her arms, to keep her prisoner, and I drop a kiss on her shoulder. This time I'm well aware of what I'm doing.

⟡

She goes to her room, I go to mine. I hear water running in the bathroom. And the springs in her bed. I think I even hear her sigh, but maybe I'm projecting.

I look at the ceiling for a long time, without moving, and I finally go to sleep I suppose, because I wake up the next morning in the same position, exactly the same position.

It takes me a while to get my brain working: I really am in Baie-Comeau, in a motel room, alone. In the room next door, also alone, is Josée. Between us, a cardboard wall. I knock three times, gently, to wake her. I picture her still drowsy, and warm, and wrapped in shreds of dreams. She's still asleep, I suppose, because it takes a while before she replies by knocking three times too, but very softly.

THE DIVE

*S*aturday morning, half-past nine. First classifications at the high school pool. Marie is there, making her way along a three-metre diving board. My little Marie who, seen from below, suddenly appears so tall, yet so fragile. She isn't looking at me — she never looks at the stands before a dive, it has to do with keeping her concentration, but I sense that she's nervous. She isn't wearing the confident smile that she usually displays when she feels ready, and her legs aren't trembling as they usually do when the muscles quiver and relax before going into action. She's not isolating herself, enclosing herself in her bubble. When she really feels ready, she has often told me, she becomes completely deaf to outside sounds, and she feels a gentle warmth sweep over her, regardless of the temperature. This morning, though, she's shivering and cold and her lips are blue. She isn't ready and she knows it, but she has to keep going. She is still hesitating when she gets to the end of the board and I can sense her whole body become taut, as if she were trying to compensate through a final effort of will — but it's too late for willpower now: at the moment when she plunges, she must on the contrary relax, let herself go, as in a dream ...

She puts all her energy into her legs, leaps very high, achieves a proper pike position — or so it seems to me, though I'm no judge — but she fails her entry into the water.

She knows that she failed at her dive, she knows much better than we do, and you can read it on her face when she gets out of the pool. She knows and she shakes her head to keep from hearing the comforting words of Amélie, who's waiting for her with a towel, or the encouraging ones of Élisabeth, though she always comes up with the necessary words.

Marie is disappointed and you can see it: she chews at her lips, gets up and paces, disturbs everyone. She's so nervous that she's annoying, so nervous that Élisabeth goes and whispers in her ear to try to calm her down, to make her look calm at any rate. Though she stays in her seat, she's still nodding her head, and her legs are wobbly.

I don't recognize my daughter. This is not the first time though that she's missed a dive, and she's always known how to react: keep quiet, breathe deeply to enclose herself in her bubble, turn the page and imagine the next dive, go back inside her bubble ... But I'm a fine one to be talking, I can't sit still on my bench even though I don't have to dive, and I squirm whenever another contestant flies into space in more and more complicated figures. How can they be so light, how can they have so much time to execute their spins, their somersaults, their reverse dives? There must be a breeze machine, there has to be some trick, otherwise it's impossible.

Maybe I shouldn't be watching. Maybe I should be thinking about something else. I turn towards Josée, who seems so calm and who is right there, close to me, so close that I can touch her. I just have to hold out my hand and I can join her in her own bubble … I'd rather go back to the divers who follow one another onto the board, who bounce, splash, swim …

"From a little distance," Josée tells me, "it seems as if they're all taking part in a big chain, in the same movement, the same ballet …"

She's right: when you look at the overall movement, the individuals disappear and the girls seem to be walking in one of those Escher drawings in which the perspectives are distorted. I finally manage to relax, at least until it's Marie's turn again. There is only her, and there's nothing I can do, no ballets, no Escher drawings. There's Marie, only Marie, who seems to me as tense as on her first try, at least until she talks to Amélie. I don't know what the two of them tell one another, but a genuine miracle occurs: they both start laughing and all at once Marie relaxes, as if she's been struck by grace. She makes her way to the diving board, climbs the ladder, and I can sense that she's radiant when she stops to clear her mind.

She shuts her eyes, concentrates, and closes herself inside her bubble so well that the silence spreads to the bleachers: I hear nothing more either, and I feel relaxed, as if time has frozen. She walks slowly to the end of the diving board, and every move breaks down into an infinite number of fixed images, into minute portions of eternity, and during one of those eternities she emerges from her bubble, something I've never seen her do. One second, barely one second to wave to Amélie from the end of the board. Amélie waves back and Marie returns to her bubble, like that, instantaneously, as if there were nothing easier than to disregard the rest of the universe. And then she dives and it's her finest dive, a one-half somersault, with a magnificent rip, an entry into the water so clean that there isn't the smallest splash. "Did a girl enter here?" the drops of water could have said. "Sorry, we didn't notice."

A perfect dive, but the coefficient of difficulty is too small. It won't be enough to win the medal. Marie knows that better than I do, yet she's radiant when she emerges from the water and rushes over to Amélie who is waiting for her with a towel.

She looks happy, she's smiling, she applauds enthusiastically when her friends succeed at complicated figures and she tries to console them when they fail. Sometimes she looks our way and waves, and it's not the same Marie, not the same little girl as a while ago, she's no longer altogether *my* little girl, and that's fine. I don't know what is going on in her head, but I do know that she's fine: I know that no matter what she's done, she's done it well.

ॐ

I have to wait till the noon break before I can actually talk to her.

"I knew I didn't have a chance of winning. So I dived for me, just for me. And I loved it … I felt relaxed … I want to go on diving but I don't want to compete any more."

"Are you sure you want to give it up?"

Between us the agreement has always been clear: as long as she wanted to continue, she could count on our support. If she wanted to give it up, the decision would be hers and hers alone. We wouldn't try to make her change her mind, but for her part, there was to be no shilly-shallying.

She didn't hesitate for a second, she nodded so straight-forwardly, so clearly, that if there'd been the slightest doubt in her little noggin, it had left via her ears.

"I'm sure."

"And are you happy?"

"I'm happy I did what I did and now I'm happy to stop."

How could I respond to that? It was her life, her decision. I just had to note it and that's that. I was relieved, to tell the truth, for her as much as for me: for her who'd no longer have to put up with all that pressure, and for me who wouldn't have to get up at dawn to go and breathe chlorine; for her who'd no longer have butterflies in her stomach as she climbed onto the diving board, and for me who'd no longer suffer cramps every time she dived. Something else would come along, another sport, another activity, but I wouldn't mind that this one was over. The future seemed simpler now, not so fraught. The present, on the other hand, had me terribly worried.

"And now what do we do?"

Apparently I've managed to communicate my concern to Marie, because I saw her smile fade, her shoulders slump, her eyes mist over. You'd have said that I'd just knocked her out of the sky — she who had just taken flight. She started talking a mile a minute, and Amélie joined her, each of them agreeing with what the other said, and outdoing her.

"We don't go home right away, we'll stay till the end, we've got our places in the school gym, it doesn't cost anything, the delegation pays for it, we'll come back on the bus with everybody else, Élisabeth takes care of everything, we want to stay with our friends, it would be mean to drop them now, there's lots of things we can do to help them, we can't go home right away, it just started ... You can if you want, but we're staying!"

And the two girls nod at the same time, defiant.

I turn towards Josée.

"What do you think?"

"If they want to stay I have no objections ... (*Yesssss!* said the girls, and me too, but silently). "The rooms are reserved in any case ... We could watch some of the competitions, check out some of the local sights ..."

The girls couldn't have cared less what we were doing. They'd got authorization to stay and nothing else mattered. We no sooner have time to agree that we would see each other now and then and the girls are off to join their friends, who are waiting to take them to the school cafeteria for lunch.

ᴖ

Josée and I didn't go for lunch that day. We'd intended to, though, when we left the pool: first we'd stop by the motel to pick up something or other — Josée's glasses, I think, but it's of no importance — then we'd intended to grab a bite to eat somewhere, and then ... and then I don't know what, and that's of no importance either.

We went by way of Josée's room where she picked up her glasses or whatever it was and we were about to go out again when there was a moment of confusion: she stopped suddenly and turned around to pick up her keys, which she'd left on the dresser, and I must have been miles away because I forgot to stop. There we were, face to face, and ... What followed was a long, a very long moment of confusion.

ᴖ

I've always thought that curtains, blinds and ellipses ought to rank very high on any list of the great innovations, along with the wheel, the plough and the printing press. While it's true that erotic scenes in movies are sometimes beautiful, it's because the bodies are perfect, the lighting painstakingly arranged, and the setting carefully chosen. What is depicted is more like dancing than sex, you mustn't confuse the genres. And if the greatest writers have fallen flat on their faces when they want to be titillating, I'm certainly not going to try. Such matters are best kept silent. They're not to be looked at, they're not to be read about, or if they are, then only in very small doses. As for living them though, they're just fine, no matter what the dose.

You already know the setting: two motel rooms so much alike that going from one to the other was like passing through a mirror. As background music, the gurgle of water in the pipes and the metallic racket from the air conditioner. Now imagine two bodies in their forties, two guilty consciences, and not a hint of a choreographer to fine-tune our movements and create the illusion of a work of art. It was very awkward, if you really want to know, awkward and self-conscious, the first time anyway — the second too for that matter — but it was Josée and me, it was her and me, it was her skin and mine, my hands and hers, and her hair and its perfumes, and all of that blending together so well that there was nothing to say, there was no need for words; only Josée and me, in her room or mine, on one side of the mirror or the other. We did practically nothing else for three days, without ever talking, without ever telling each other anything, as if silence guaranteed us anonymity, as if we were anyone at all, as if we were ageless.

We went out now and then to eat or say hi to the girls at the pool, and we'd drop in at the arena now and then to pretend we were following some of the competitions, but we never stayed long. We preferred to wander aimlessly through the streets of Baie-Comeau, and don't ask me to name a single one of them or to describe any landscape whatsoever. I didn't feel in the least like a tourist. Josée brushes my hand, I drop a kiss on her shoulder, and soon we're kissing in a Tim Horton's parking lot and we can hardly restrain ourselves till we're back at the motel.

To walk aimlessly through the streets of Baie-Comeau, and feel excitement overwhelming us, and go back as fast as possible to one or the other of the rooms that are really one, and tear off our clothes, and find ourselves in a bed, and feel as if we're at the same time sixteen years old and forty, and start over again and again to make up for all that lost time, saying nothing but seeking out one another, exploring one another in every way we can, for as long as we can, until we're falling asleep; and then to fall asleep with no idea of the time, and wake up, and start again, each time more gently, each time more violently, each time more desperately, and start again one last time on Tuesday morning while we're packing, just before we go to say goodbye to the girls, whom we've caught as they were boarding their bus, and another last time in a wooded area near Les Escoumins, and a final last time in the car, just after the big hill at Sainte-Anne-de-Beaupré, when we feel as if we are landing back in real life, after a long journey in the clouds.

ᦔ

"And now what do we do?" she asked then (unless it was me).

"No idea," I replied (unless it was her).

"Did you tell?"

"Tell what?"

"Amélie didn't spend a single night in the motel, the communicating rooms ... Did you tell, when you phoned?"

"No. It didn't seem like a good ... Did you?"

"Me neither ... Couldn't we decide that it's best not to say anything for another little while? Let some time pass, see what happens, not rush matters ... We don't say anything, okay? We don't say anything and we give ourselves a week to think things over ..."

But others were going to do the thinking in our place, and remind us that we can't always invent the endings that we'd like.

ᦔ

It's been a long time since we've said anything. After Quebec City, our bubble burst on the hard edges of reality, and we content ourselves with looking straight ahead at the road, trying to understand what happened and to guess what is going to happen next. We are on our way back to the real world, we're going to resume our old habits, but I feel as if I'm heading for the unknown. My throat is so dry that I have trouble swallowing. I bend over now and then to watch the kilometres roll along on the odometer and I have the impression that someone must have tampered with it: I can't believe that this distance, usually so boring, is passing so quickly. The Montérégie mountains already. On the horizon, Mount Royal, downtown...

Since Quebec City, I no longer dare to touch her hand when she shifts gears, and certainly not to stroke her thigh. Her throat is as dry as mine, it seems, because she has to cough slightly two or three times before she can say something, around Mont Saint-Hilaire. I assume that she's going to say something, that she's going to repeat that it's best to say nothing, and to give ourselves some time, but she sings, rather she murmurs a few notes: "From as far back as the shadows, my old loves come back to me."

Together, we sing her favourite songs, the ones she loves best. Well, "sing" may be an exaggeration. We whisper, rather. Never has my voice been so hoarse, never have I sung so off-key, never has my off-key singing been so eloquent.

"The road was long, but I travelled that long road..."

"Thank you," she says when we catch sight of the trees in the extraordinary garden and we're gradually approaching my street. Thank you, whatever happens. Thanks to Barbara, to the singers, the composers, the musicians, thank you for all those portable bubbles ...

I look at Josée one last time, when we pull up in front of my house: she has succeeded in astonishing me one more time. That's most likely the quality of hers that I'd miss the most. Through her tears, despite the fact that she had never believed in God, and just when we least expected it, she always found a place for gratitude.

WHAT DO WE DO NOW?

*M*arie-France is outside when we arrive. She has just come home from work, but she's had enough time to remove her disguise — the costume of an insurance company's model employee — and change into jeans and T-shirt and go out to the backyard, barefoot in the grass, as she loves to do during a heat wave: bare feet on the cool earth — the best air-conditioning system.

She sees Josée's car stop in front of the house, walks up to it and right away, before the engine is even turned off, she guesses everything there is to guess. It has to do with the way I look at her through the windshield a little at a time, and even more, from the way that Josée doesn't look at her at all.

When I get out of the car I'm numb, and it's not from driving too long. Everything gives me away, everything, from the way I move to my overly polite goodbye to Josée before she goes home, to the unusual enthusiasm I show Cléo, who doesn't stop licking me, to the kiss that I finally give Marie-France, feeling horribly awkward. It took just a few days for my hands and my arms to adapt to Josée's measurements: I'm surprised to find that Marie-France is so slim, so delicate. Her scents are disconcerting, her hair too soft and strangely silky; even the texture of her skin seems new to me, as if Marie-France were the one I didn't know, as if it were Marie-France whom I was touching for the first time, though I've known her for more than twenty years. I feel like a child who's kissing his cousin and is ignorant of the protocol: am I supposed to keep my lips on that skin or am I supposed to break away? I feel improper and I know that I'll feel just as improper in the days and weeks to come, and in the months and years to follow, and to the very end. I know that nothing will be as it was before, no matter what I say and no matter what I do.

I'm a bundle of uneasiness, from the tips of my toes to the ends of my hair. There's not one pore in my skin that doesn't ooze guilt. How could Marie-France not have seen it, not have sensed it, she who has known me for so long, she who has just been waiting for *that*?

She has guessed everything, but she doesn't say a word. Not right away. First we try to resume our daily routine, to find our way onto the terrain of the reassuringly trivial: your mother phoned, the hydro bill came, Cléa was sick, maybe we should take her to the vet…

I've always liked those words that we hear without hearing them, those remarks that we respond to with absent-minded muttering, though they're the most important ones. The words of the poor, as Léo Ferré would say: "Don't come home too late, be careful you don't catch cold"… Marie-France talks about everyday matters while we sit in the yard, and finally I can relax a little.

"Any word from Mathieu?"

"I called the camp, everything's fine. He went to the infirmary twice. Once for a scrape, once because he lost his voice from yelling…"

"Did you talk to him?"

"It's not allowed. If all the kids talked to their parents there'd be no end to it … He's coming home Saturday, as planned."

I would have liked to go on talking about Mathieu and Marie, about Cléo and Cléa, about the hydro bill and the dead leaves piling up in the eavestrough, or about the lawn, or about anything. The more we talk about the house, the more I feel that I'm back in touch with reality, the more I'm able to believe that it's possible to say nothing, to pretend that nothing happened, to believe that time will sort out everything. Dead leaves are accumulating in the eavestroughs — I'll clean them out, and then it will be winter, and spring will return, and I'll start washing the windows, cutting the grass, taking the kids to the pool or the rink, and that's all. Weekdays, I'll go to work, and every time I'll come home a little more tired, and it will be just fine, it will be the life I've chosen. Marie-France will be there, as always; she may know everything but she will say nothing, because it's better that way, we'll pretend so convincingly that we'll finally believe ourselves, we'll forget ...

"What do we do now?"

This time I know perfectly well who spoke first. Marie-France is sitting in her Adirondack chair, legs folded under her, totally concentrating on the glass of white wine that she is twirling pensively in her fingers. We've had time to talk about Marie, who doesn't regret her decision to give up diving, and I was about to deliver some platitudes about Baie-Comeau when she came out with her question.

For a minute I'm dumbstruck, asking myself if I ought to feign surprise in an attempt to gain some time, or pretend to be indignant by denying everything, or simply confess ...

"Look, let's stop pretending nothing happened," she says, looking me squarely in the eyes. "It was bound to happen one day or another ... And what do we do now?"

I try to speak, even though I've never been so confused, even though I've never felt so strongly that words have no meaning. Maybe that attempt will help me to understand, you never know ... I try to say something, sticking as closely to the truth as possible, but all I do is stammer, go in circles. I call on the inevitable accident, talk about the series of coincidences that followed, even biology, claim it was just one of those things: most likely anybody under such circumstances ... The more I say, the harder it is for me to believe myself: if it isn't just one of those things, whispers my little inner voice, then it's the most wonderful mistake you've ever made. The truth is that you have no regrets, none at all. There isn't one minute of those three days with Josée that you wouldn't live over, again and again, and it's Josée you're thinking about now, even though it should be Marie-France.

"Just one of those things?" Marie-France repeats, thoughtfully. "Just one of those things that's been in the works for ages ... Do you really expect me to believe that?"

We're interrupted by the telephone: the girls' bus has arrived, they're waiting for us in the school parking lot.

"I'll go if you want," says Marie-France. "You must be tired ..."

She goes inside for her keys and sunglasses, and I sit there, stunned, watching her walk to the car, amazed yet again to see how delicate, how vulnerable she is. She must be as overwhelmed as I am, yet she seems so flexible, so light, so fluid. While I feel weighed down with guilt, as if leather straps are holding me in my lawn chair, as if the feet of my chair were sinking deep into the earth.

My own feet are screwed into the grass, my arms stuck to the chair. Only my head is moving, very slowly, while I take a panoramic look around the yard: I study every brick, every plank, every shingle, as if my mind wants to appropriate them forever. That maple at the back of the yard, that branch over which Marie used to toss a blanket to make a tent for herself. The maple that you planted, that you've watched grow, change colour, die every fall and come back to life every spring, and that chipped cement on the foundation where Mathieu and Alexandre used to practise their slap shots, and the bikes in the shed, and the basketball net you were finally able to put up — no, there's no garage, we can't have everything, but still, there's a pole where I was able to put a net at regulation height — and the drool-soaked ball that Cléo persists in bringing you, that you pretend not to see, and the rose bushes that Marie-France covers with burlap every autumn and that you bury in snow when you shovel the driveway, making igloos that will protect them from freezing: all that you risk losing, Marc-André, all those little things that sum up the happy family you never knew, that you tried to build one stone, one plank, one moment at a time, to give to your children. And even if it wasn't a happy family, even if it was simply a normal family, an ordinary family, the most ordinary of ordinary families, what right do you have to break it?

"Hi papa!" says Marie, whom I've barely had time to notice. She has raced to her room where she's very likely phoning Amélie: it's been five minutes since they parted, they must have a million things to tell one another.

I finally manage to get up and I go directly to Marie-France.

"I want you to believe me," I tell her before she has time to say a word. "That's what I want. I want you to believe me when I tell you that it was just one of those things …"

She doesn't reply right away. Not directly, at any rate. The conversation takes an inexplicable, unexpected turn: what Marie-France talks about now is golf. That's right, golf. She's going to have to take lessons, she tells me. Everybody at work plays, the company even reimburses the fees for joining a club, people keep telling her that's where business gets done, where contracts get signed; beyond a certain level in the hierarchy, you simply can't avoid it … She's already bought golf shoes and she asks me to come and see them.

And so I go to our bedroom and look at her golf shoes, I pretend to take an interest in the seams and the studs, I even ask some questions about the cost of joining various clubs.

While I'm in the bedroom I unpack, without bothering to sort my clothes: they'll all go in the wash, it's simpler. On my way to the bathroom I notice Marie, glued to the telephone. Lying on the floor she chats away, twisting the cord around her finger as if she wants to reduce the space between her and the person on the other end, to whom she's describing her last dive. It's not Amélie then, or Maude, or any of her friends from the diving team … Who else could it be? I've long ago stopped trying to keep track of her friends. In the living room, there's a leather sofa that cost a small fortune, and a matching armchair, but Marie lies on the floor to talk on the phone. Stay young, Marie, please, stay young.

In the bathroom I notice Cléa, lying on the laundry basket. Cléa adores the bathroom, especially the cover of the wicker basket from which she can see everything: drops of water sliding down the shower curtain, the tap from which she'll take a drink, the toilet paper that she likes to unroll when she's feeling playful.

"What's the matter, Cléa?"

Cats enjoy pity and Cléa gives me a miserable look, her eyes half closed as if she wants me to go on feeling sorry for her.

"Terribly sorry, Cléa, but you're going to have to get up."

She pretends she doesn't understand. I try to lift the cover off the basket without disturbing her, but I can't do it and she stalks out of the bathroom, furious. Sick, that cat? No way. She's never been so feline, so princely — I'd say princessly if the word existed.

Then we eat outside, all three of us; we talk about Marie's dives and the squirrels that keep challenging Cléo (they're driving the poor dog crazy), about school, which starts soon, about skirts and the school bus, lunch boxes and the dishwasher, which is leaving streaks on the glasses...

I keep myself a little outside the conversation and I steal a look at Marie-France whenever I can. It really does seem as if nothing has happened, as if life is continuing its course, as if it's flowing along in its bed as naturally as anything, without ever overflowing, without ever going outside the lines.

And then we go to the video store to rent a film. A Jane Austenish story, with beautiful gowns for the girls and Michelle Pfeiffer for me. Don't ask me what the title was, or what it was about. Michelle Pfeiffer was in it, that I'm sure of, and there was me getting up every now and then for popcorn or mineral water, and every time I touched something, I couldn't get over the fact that the thing existed and that it was so straightforward. Yes, it's a plastic bowl, and yes, you're really walking in your own house, on your own kitchen floor … That feeling of strangeness, like when you return from a long trip. To be at home but feel as if you're in a dream, in a parallel universe where you don't know the codes.

Rewind the film, get ready for bed, think the toothpaste tastes odd, wash my hands much longer than usual, feel as if I reek of strange smells, hesitate before looking at myself in the mirror, finally take a chance on it and discover an aged, hunched, wrinkled man. Yet only yesterday I was sixteen years old …

Marie-France is in bed waiting for me, pretending she's reading a novel. Her blue pyjamas, her glasses at the end of her nose; all around her, pillows, cushions, flowered sheets; she has always known how to create clouds around us.

She puts a bookmark in her novel and starts talking to me even before I get under the covers. I lie as close to the edge as possible in order to avoid any contact, but how can you not touch a woman when you've shared her bed, and all you have to do is move the covers and her perfumes awaken and caress you? I settle on my side, with my back against two pillows, and I listen to her talk about Marie, about her way of experimenting, of moving on to something else with no regrets, apparently, at any rate, about Mathieu who's more of a worrier and a perfectionist, beneath a cooler exterior …

Then I talk about their temperaments, about the way that each of them approaches the world, about their different ways of skating or diving, and I'm almost able to be there, just there, with no other thoughts at the back of my mind, without a corner of my brain wondering, at the same time that the words are coming out of my mouth, what exactly is going on in Marie-France's mind. What game is she playing? Is she really playing at being the one who doesn't see or hear anything, does she think it will be easier for her to forget if we never talk about it again?

"I'm willing to try," she says finally when I am least expecting her to broach the subject. "I'm willing to try to believe you. The question is, do you believe yourself…"

And then she switches off the light and turns over to sleep — to try, anyway — and I turn on my side to watch as the night slowly grows thinner until it's daytime again.

Do I believe myself, do I know what it is that I want?

I want Marie-France and I want Josée. I want Josée again and again, and even if I don't want her, I just have to look at her and I want her in spite of myself, but I couldn't bear to break up with Marie-France and Marie and Mathieu, I want Marie-France and Marie and Mathieu, I want us all together, but I couldn't bear to lose Josée … Stories don't end the way you want, no, that would be too easy, especially when you don't even know what ending you yearn for.

Objects are emerging from the half-light one by one while the night is being diluted, and there I am with my eyes levelled at the telephone. At the other end, at the end of an inextricable network of circuits, she is there, Josée is there ... I would just have to go down to the living room, punch in her number. We agreed not to phone one another for a week, but I can tell that I won't make it, that I won't be able to resist. Maybe if I wound the cord around my finger, maybe if I thought about her very hard, maybe the circuits would finally blend together ... How are you doing?

OFFSIDE

I've never been so relieved to go to work as I am that week. I almost wish for traffic jams on the Jacques-Cartier bridge: one foot on the brake, the other on the gas, advance one metre every half-hour, at least that's one thing I can do without hurting anyone. Listen to the radio, fight exasperation by letting my mind wander, look at the powder house on St. Helen's Island and tell myself that it will last longer than the pavilions built for Expo 67, turn my head towards the roller coasters at La Ronde — what evolutionary aberration has led certain animals to pay for a fright? — scrutinize every screw, every nut and bolt in the steel structure, and ask myself if we can really trust engineers, and think about Josée and about Marie-France, about Marie-France and about Josée, over and over again, and advance one more metre … How is it that resources were found for building bridges during the 1960s, and for digging a subway system, and creating islands, while today not a cent can be found for their upkeep? Above all, how is it that humanity can produce engineers wonderfully able to calculate the resistance of materials, yet a person can feel so helpless when he spends a few days in Baie-Comeau and then tries to understand what happened? Move forward one more metre, try to take an interest in the sports news, guess from the sound of his voice that the reporter may be having marital problems too, yet he's doing his job all the same, as conscientiously as possible, because it's still the best way to busy himself and maybe even to recover. Los Angeles 8, Chicago 4. Detroit 6, Toronto 5. He's probably talking about baseball. When the numbers are in the teens, it's football. Close to a hundred, basketball. And when it's millions, then they're talking about salaries … Beside me, a driver is taking advantage of the traffic jam to iron out some problems on his cell phone. I'd like to borrow it and call Josée: how are you doing? But have you ever seen someone *lend* his cell phone, thereby admitting that he has *a little* spare time and he's not *completely* indispensable? Move forward another metre, imagine that I'm climbing onto the roller coaster and that I'm trying to communicate with Josée through telepathy: I know, we said that we'd wait a week, but I could never hold out that long. How are you doing?

I finally get to the office, where I carry out my duties as conscientiously as I can. I try to lose myself in my work, to drown in it. Bring them on: contracts to sign, taxes to calculate, additions to check, clauses to study. I get through a lot of work, I level mountains, I'm a titan of productivity, a Stakhanovite of the public service. Entrust me with the national debt, I'll eliminate it for you. The only things I really can't bear are meetings: as soon as the arguments start getting repeated even a little, I switch off, I leave for the clouds again, I look for a telephone. How are you doing?

I don't like meetings and I don't like coffee breaks and I particularly don't like lunch hour. I don't care for the dull, desultory conversations about someone-or-other's brother-in-law who has cancer even though he managed to quit smoking, or someone else who wants to get a new car, and I definitely don't want to know about election rumours and their repercussions on budget allocations. Give me numbers please, contracts to check, columns to add up, give me files that I can drown in.

The first day passes and I can cope. I go home at six-thirty, I put the dishes away and I walk the dog, I play with the kids and I watch TV, I cut the grass and I change the kitty litter. Bring on the domestic tasks, bring on the household and its obligations, and could you please stop the phone from ringing? Every time, I jump, every time, my heart stops beating. How are you doing? But it's never her.

I cope for three days and then I can't take it any more. I find some pretext for leaving the office, I go to the nearest pay phone and I look up the number of one of the two schools where she works.

"The library, please."

I drum on the glass while I wait for my call to be transferred, and all at once I stop: what if somebody sees me? Above all, don't attract attention, try to make as little noise as possible, try not to stand out … What are you worried about, man? That the cops will arrest you and lock you up because you're phoning a woman with whom you committed the terrible crime of adultery? It's a horrible word, true, but you aren't risking jail or the lash … The phone rings three times and already I have palpitations. Maybe she isn't there. Maybe it's the wrong school …

"Hello?"

It's her. I had one chance in two of getting the right school on my first try, but I'm still surprised to hear her voice. It's her, I'm sure of it, but at the same time I don't recognize her: her voice sounds flat, distant. It sounds as if she's talking through a handkerchief, like a bandit demanding a ransom in an old movie.

"Hello?" she says again.

"Hello, it's me …"

How could she recognize me? I have no idea: I didn't recognize myself. Never has my voice been so weak, so dry.

"We'd said that …"

"I can't wait. I just want to know how you're doing, I want to know if …"

"I'm not doing very well. Robert knows. Making up stories was pointless. He just had to look at me and he knew. I don't know what's going to happen now, but … Look, we won't speak any more, okay? We won't see each other, we'll stop phoning. It's over, okay?"

"No."

"Look, we have to …"

"No. Now listen to me: you've got an hour for lunch? We have to see each other, we have to talk at least once … Robert won't know a thing … Just once …"

༈

So we saw each other one last time, that very day. In August, 1993. Seven years ago, precisely seven. I went to her school in Saint-Lambert. As the school year hadn't started yet, the area around it was deserted, and we simply went to the football field and sat in the bleachers.

She looks so distraught, her features so drawn that I have trouble recognizing her. It's been three days since I've seen her, but she looks as if she hasn't slept for three months. She's shattered, she seems drained of her substance. She's been in pain, she's been afraid …

The thought brushed my mind, I confess. Never would I have thought Robert capable of such a thing, but still I study her face, her arms: no marks, none.

"I didn't have to tell him," she repeats. "He figured it out …"

"Marie-France too … It's better that way, I think."

I talk to her about Marie-France, she talks to me about Robert, sometimes we talk at the same time, but it's to say the same things, in the same words, and we fall silent at the same time, and we start talking again at the same time to tell each other that it makes no sense, that we've been reckless, that we had no right to cause such pain, that the children would never understand, that we had no right...

We talk a little while longer, trying not to look in one another's eyes, trying instead to watch an imaginary football game on the deserted field. It's nothing but an imaginary game, played by invisible players, but it's the most violent thing I've ever seen. There are the white lines freshly drawn in chalk, and we talk about the rules to respect, about lines to stay inside: even if the pass is incredible and the catch spectacular, even if it's the best play of the game and maybe even of the decade, it's worthless if the player is off side. Inside the lines, it's okay. Two centimetres more and it's offside. That's the way it is. It's the rule. The referee blows his whistle, we try to forget, and we start over again. The pass was quite simply not made. It has no more weight than a dream.

"Are you sure that's what you want? To respect the regulations, stay inside the lines... Are you sure that's what you want?"

"Yes, I'm sure..."

"Really? Say it again. Repeat it three times. Repeat it three times, I swear that I'll never phone your place again, I swear that I'll never try to see you again, I swear that you'll never hear from me again."

"I'm sure, I'm sure..."

Her voice breaks and she can't go on. Or maybe she was able to say it and I didn't hear. Maybe she only whispered it, or she said it inwardly but it counts all the same. I don't know, I never did know and I never will know. She gets up and returns to her school without looking back, without turning around.

I watch her until the door closes on her. I stay in the bleachers for a moment, watching the sparrows, which know nothing about regulations, and which touch down on the field to swipe blades of grass, and then I stand up, I return to my car, I cross the bridge one more time, and I go back to work. Let's say rather, I go back to the office.

CREDITS

One week later. A Friday evening, the last one before the first day of school. Marie-France and Just Plain Marie have gone shopping at the mall. Mathieu and I are alone at home and we've rented a film from the video store. It's one of those films Mathieu loves, where the heroes travel to the borders of the remotest galaxies and find themselves in a universe that strangely resembles Europe in the Middle Ages. I don't actually hate that kind of film myself. Since you can guess the whole story as soon as the credits come up, you can sit back quietly in your favourite armchair and deprogram yourself for a while. Since it's raining buckets and I don't feel like going for a walk, it will be an adequate substitute. No sooner has the film started than the phone rings.

"Should I put it on pause?" asks Mathieu when I get up to answer.

"That's okay, keep it running…"

I pick up the phone.

"Hello, it's Robert."

Thanks be to God, Mathieu's spaceship has already entered hyperspace where a first regiment of sidereal gargoyles is waiting. My son can't see then that I'm scarlet.

"Hi Robert. I …"

"Listen to me, Marc, and listen carefully, I'm only going to say this once."

He whispers rather than talks, but I don't miss a word. His voice is so metallic, so cold, that it penetrates deep into my bones.

"I've just got one thing to say to you and I'm going to say it on the phone because it's better for you. I could have killed you. It would've been easy. I thought about it. I could kill you even now but I'm not going to: I've got too much respect for the children. I hope that I'll never see you again, Marc-André."

He hangs up and I stand there for a long time listening to the dial tone.

Then I go back to sit in my armchair and I watch the images stream past.

"That was good, eh papa?"

"What? Is it over already? I lost some bits I think … I was miles away…"

"We can watch it again if you want…"

"No, that's okay. I think I'll take it back to the video store right now. Cléo needs a walk."

"Can I come too?"

"In the rain?"

"I don't mind," he says, shrugging. "I'm not made of chocolate."

Thank you, Mathieu. Thank you for being there, thank you for walking in the rain with me, and thank you for not asking any questions when I told you that I might not be your hockey coach next season, because … because every now and then we need a change, that's all …

JUSTICE DENIED

$\mathcal{T}$here was no hockey that year, and Mathieu took it well.

"If Robert isn't the coach I'm not interested. The others are too weird. I like judo better, I've decided. When do we put our names down?"

"Okay for judo, but why'd you say 'we'? Surely you aren't expecting me to become a judo coach!"

"Judo coach? You? Hardly," he says, laughing. (Why is he laughing, for that matter? Why does the thought strike him as *that* ridiculous?) "But you'll still have to get up on Saturday morning."

"That's fine. I'm curious to have a look at judo lessons … I don't imagine there'll be any noisemakers in the bleachers …"

"Why did they go away, papa?"

It's the same thing every time. Whenever we go walking in the extraordinary garden, or when we walk Cléo in the neighbourhood. Or when we drive in the area around Alexandre's house. Every time he asks me the same question: how come they left?

I always give him the same answer: Robert's a policeman and policemen are often asked to move. That's the way it is. They don't really have to, but...

"It isn't fair."

"In Quebec City, Robert will have a higher salary and he thought it would be better for his family... I'm sure he thought about his family, that he acted for the best ..."

That's cheating a little: true, he thought it would be better for his family, but money wasn't involved. In fact he didn't get a promotion and he sacrificed his house, which he sold very quickly without waiting to get his asking price.

"Look at Cléo! He still wants to go there!"

We just have to turn onto that street and Cléo, nose to the sidewalk, leads us straight to the house where he recognizes so many smells. He had friends who lived there not all that long ago, and familiar smells ... How can you explain to a dog that a house can changes masters, and that the ones who bought this one — an elderly couple with no children — aren't thieves or usurpers? It's their house now, Cléo, they're settling in with their own smells, you see ...

"It's unfair," says Mathieu again, as we continue on our way. "Will we be able to go and see them in Quebec City?"

"Sure, of course …"

Sure, of course … Adults' words, parents' words, words that children never believe altogether: tomorrow, later on, when you're a grown-up …

And Cléo looks at the house again, he looks at the usurper planting something or other in the flower beds, and you can sense that he's confused: what's that woman doing there? He'd like to bark, to say get out of there, he'd like to say it's unfair, he'd like to ask why doesn't everything change back to the way it was before, why can't we make up the endings that we want?

I'm projecting of course. Why else do we have animals?

～

Sometimes there were letters from Quebec City in the mailbox, and Mathieu was excited: a letter from Alex, a letter from Alex!

But it didn't last long. It's complicated, writing. And it will never replace the sound of a puck on the blue line, the smell of wet grass, the feel of a leather football …

Mathieu made other friends, but no one replaced Alex, no one will ever replace him. Actually, the word is a strange one. As if one friend could replace another, as if they were employees on an assembly line … Mathieu made other friends, but he never got over Alex. For him, as for us, it was a wonderful period, a wonderful time. We made some fine memories for him, memories he can always dip into during the most difficult moments. There was that basketball net in the yard, remember? And what about the year we nearly won the championship …

Mathieu is seventeen now. He still sniffs his toast in the morning.

ᠵ

Just Plain Marie and Amélie never stopped corresponding. They visited each other now and then, travelling by bus, and even by car. The shock I had when I saw Amélie drive onto our street at the wheel of her Honda! Amélie is a gorgeous young woman who's studying medicine, as I've already told you, I think. We see her arrive at our house once or twice a year. The two girls shut themselves away in Marie's room, where they comb their ponies. They were there just last week.

"And how's your mother, Amélie? How are your parents?"

"They're well, very well …"

I'd have liked to sequester her there and squeeze her like a lemon, ask her tons of questions, ask if her mother still knows all of Barbara's songs by heart, if she still puts all kinds of blue in her colouring books, if she reads fat novels in bed at night, if her hands are still cool, if there's an extraordinary garden near her place, if she has beautiful lines at the corners of her eyes, and if she still tells ideal stories, if her imagination takes her walking through the streets of Baie-Comeau, if she thinks about me now and then … But I do nothing of the kind. I ask, "How's your mother, how are your parents?" in a detached tone, and I look nearly abstracted when I hear her answer: "They're fine, they're really fine."

After that I have days to ponder her reply, when I'm walking along the paths on Mount Royal.

No, I don't go there with Cléo. He's dead. Golden retrievers are sturdy but at the same time they're terribly fragile. When they start having problems with their hips …

We didn't replace him. And we live in the city now, of course. Cross the bridge every day, morning and night: we finally got the picture.

So I was saying that every time I ponder Amélie's reply for days. What exactly does that mean, they're fine? That Josée's health is good and that everything is going pretty well the way she wants, or does it mean that she's happy? That's what I hope, of course, even if …

What would I do if I knew she was unhappy, if I learned that she's separated, that she isn't with Robert? Would I phone her, would I dare to show up at her place saying, here I am, it's been seven years since we've seen each other, but that was just a pause, a hiatus …

Let's talk instead about the imagination, is that okay? Let's talk instead about those images that, for seven years, were waiting for me at every turn, at every bend in the path. She was there, a silent, smiling figure who didn't say a word and continued along her way. Or else I was filling up at a self-service gas station I didn't usually go to, I was digging around in my wallet for my debit card, and there she was, in front of me, she'd just turned around after paying, we nearly bumped into each other, there we were, less than a foot from each other, so close that I could smell her perfumes ... Or else I was at a roadside stop and there she was, buying a chocolate bar from the vending machine. Or else at the movies, at the mall, at the side of the road, everywhere in fact, and any time — but most of all when I was crossing the bridge and an old French song was playing on the radio. I resented her a little for having contaminated half of the French repertoire, to tell the truth. And I gazed at her face, which took up so much room that it became confused with the sky.

In the beginning she was there, everywhere, every day, several times a day. With time, of course, I came to think about her less often. With time, sure ...

And what would I say to her now, seven years later? I'd tell her that she no longer fills the whole sky, no, only part of it. And I'd thank her for having used her Prismacolor to draw me such beautiful skies, and I'd even thank her three times rather than one, so that my recollection of her would lodge in three different parts of my memory and I would never forget her.

ACKNOWLEDGEMENTS

I am grateful to the Canada Council for the Arts for its encouragement;

to Robert Malenfant for telling me about the world of federal civil servants;

to Guylaine Jutras, Nicolas Arsenault, Josée Saint-Antoine, and Paul Décarie for taking such good fictional care of Amélie; to Donald Normand and Élisabeth Paquin of the Quebec Diving Federation, who didn't bat an eyelid when I twisted the truth by setting the Baie-Comeau Games during the summer rather than the winter; to Jules, who showed me how to breathe in the smell of my toast; to Jean-Marie Poupart, Suzanne Beauchemin, Diane Martin, Normand de Bellefeuille, Isabelle Longpré, and Anne-Marie Villeneuve for their corrections, suggestions, and encouragement; to Michèle Marineau, for her corrections, her comments, her suggestions, her smiles, her *bons mots*, in a word for pretty well everything; and finally, to the readers who've agreed to share this stretch of the road with me.